PLENARY INDULGENCE

PLENARY INDULGENCE

Ten Stories

ANNE O'BRIEN

AO Publishing

To Camille, my other "first."

CONTENTS

CHAPTER 1

Plenary Indulgence

Margaret Boyle was suffering from a curioures combination of angst and sluggishness brought on by too many cocktails the night before. She was becoming almost catatonic trying to decide whether to stay home and risk an overdraft or spend half her day on a bus. She had purchased some candy at Walgreens on Monday afternoon and damn, if she wasn't two dollars overdrawn. The decision was made when a ghoulish looking man with darting pupils was advertising debt consolidation on TV.

Margaret - or Missy as she was called in her Chicago days - was still in a quandary as she shuffled to the bathroom. She was constantly pondering the subject of money or rather her lack of it and the 'dunderheads' that could afford those new monstrosities across Flamingo Blvd. She had a litany of thorns in her side. Mixing idioms she referred to them as craws in her side and her craws were increasing by the year.

She would be shocked to know that she was a thorn to others as well. She spent hours on the phone with sincere technicians who tended to their customers with the zeal of Peace Corp volunteers. Missy had no patience with the deliberate, gentle questions and hissed a litany of obscenities when asked for serial numbers and icons off her computer. Sometimes she resorted to more expensive house calls from a service called the Geek Squad and would stand behind them and hiss at their backs, her nervous rancid breath breathing down their callow necks as they worked.

If she had chosen to take her chances and stay home on this particular Tuesday morning her alternative would have been the pool and she hated the pool. The old women never swam or smiled. They stood in a circle like bobble heads protecting hair that resembled dust bunnies and talking endlessly about either illness and eating. The old men had bodies resembling melting snow cliffs and played cards all afternoon under the cabana. The internet had described Hibiscus Hamlet as a place for "cultivating new horizons in the tropics." The ad had featured a man resembling George Clooney and a sinewy blond in a white blouse with a turned up collar and blue cotton shorts sitting on a sailboat laughing their asses off. Missy had not seen cotton, sinewy or laughter since she left Chicago.

Today Missy chose lime green Capri's and a t-shirt decorated with poodles drinking martinis, a gift from her niece Cyndi which Missy felt was way off base. She tucked a plastic baggie with five dollars in her bra. She would catch the shuttle which she referred to as a Fisher Price bus that stopped at the corner of her unit at five minutes to the hour. After the bank she'd go to the mall and use her new credit card decorated in palm trees.

She'd get something with a "little pizzazz" at Burdines. At the very least she'd buy her weekly Enquirer.

When the bus pulled up in front of Publix grocery store Janelle, the driver, made her usual stop for a cigarette break. One of the regulars accompanied her. She couldn't recall her name except that it reminded her of something you'd see engraved on the collar of a teacup dog. Today she was wearing a shirt with 'Foxy Lady' embroidered in pink rhinestones. When the bus started again she continued the ongoing saga of her horrific life.

"I have to get some rats for my snake and then I'm telling that son of a bitch Randy to get packing. He picked me up at work last night shit faced. Dee, my boss, told him to get the hell out of Snackin' Pantry and he grabbed her ass."

"Well you're better off." Janelle continued with her usual response. "The Lord writes straight with crooked lines."

Janelle drove maniacally but slowed down for any creature that was not human. At Lazy Lane Trailer Park she allowed a family of iguanas to cross. The largest looked at the bus with the squinting reproach of one whose home had been ravaged by malls and developments. A man in his late 60's with a ponytail and leathery skin got on. He was wearing a tie dyed t- shirt and tattered cargo shorts. Missy had seen a lot of his type, retirees living on nothing. They take free water color classes or learn how to make hats from palm fronds at a community center and call themselves artists. But she preferred his type to Mr. Brodky, the president of her condo association who perused the grounds every day in a golf cart in pastel polo shirts, polyester slacks snapped almost at his chest with a menacing looking white plastic belt and an expression of smelling garbage.

By the time she reached Sun Tides Bank and deposited her money Missy felt like she'd been more on an expedition then an errand. She stopped at the Walgreens by the Fashion Mall to purchase the Enquirer and pills that promised to "electrify the body." She sat on a bench inside the mall and watched South Florida's cast of characters; minuscule blonds with silicone breasts, the exotic Columbians and the usual splay legged porcine bodies. She recognized her family walking through the parking lot towards the revolving doors

"Oh God! Look who's coming and I don't want to talk." Missy was in a stew. "She's in that same blue velour outfit and if she thinks that makes her look slim she's crazy. Annie's following behind with a puss mouth and talking on that damn cell phone. Mother would die if she saw her granddaughter and twelve year old great granddaughter looking like that. Who lets a young girl wear shorts with an orange that says 'Squeeze me' on their butt?"

Missy and her sister Cecelia had been raised in an Irish Catholic household in Chicago's Rogers Park. Catholic Chicagoans referred to their neighborhood by its parish. Theirs was St Ignatius. At one time the Boyle family would have been described as lace curtain Irish. They managed to remain steadfastly on a precipice of financial calamity. They had a tea cart and sent their kids to Catholic schools and had the priest for Sunday dinners and they had their lace curtains.

Celia had the peaked complexion and cheery red lips of martyrs on holy cards. Her obedience bordered on levitation. And every nun took credit for this fragile wisp of a girl who always looked as though she was atoning for the sins of her classmates. Missy felt compelled to like her but secretly the haunted white face reminded her of those tortured spirits in horror films who peer out of tower windows. She loved to whisper obscenities to her and watch Celia's eyes roll heavenward in agonized rapture.

Missy thought it a real miracle that Celia lived through childhood in spite of her delicate nature and daily playground torture. She attributed this to her fear of germs and avoidance of anything outside of her family and her few Catholic "chums" which were mostly nuns. Celia was even given the rare privilege of calling nuns by their real names. Sister Pious Peter was Sister Patty to whom she recited her daily plenary indulgence.

Even their stern father deferred to Celia. He had a fastidious protectiveness over his fragile angel. Missy believed she was his superstitious claim to Grace, a compensation for refusing to attend Mass on Sundays. Living with Celia was a spiritual task in itself and an amulet for warding off Purgatory. Therefore It was particularly disconcerting when Celia returned home after a high school dance with face aglow like she'd finally had the Divine calling but instead poured a Coke and raved about Forest Archer. The name frightened her parents. It certainly was not Irish.

One Saturday evening several months later Missy was sitting on her chenille bedspread putting pin curls in her hair when she heard sobs coming from the dining room. Unless there was a family crisis no one sat at the Duncan Phyfe table on a week night. After several guttural "sons of a bitch and horses ass" followed by silence Missy had her own Divine moment of exultation. Even the pin curls were hot. Her mother was speaking in soft reassuring tones "Everything will be ok, dear. God help us. She can wear a tasteful white shift. God help us!"

Could it be? Their gentle fawn whose little hands shook like apple blossoms at the slightest hint of carnality was knocked up? Missy was joyful. Imagining Celia "doing it" was harder to comprehend than a Virgin Birth. This was a girl who blushed when the word brassiere was mentioned and covered her sacred crotch with cotton rosebud panties.

Forest looked like a character out of her nursery rhyme books. He was tall in a gangly invasive way with a large head and stick out ears. He was always blowing on his glasses and wiping them with his cotton handkerchief. Missy would watch them from their third floor flat as they walked towards Devon Ave and wonder if other people found them an odd couple, Celia was slightly pigeon toed and minced tentatively down the street like someone who had been recently institutionalized. Forest walked stiff legged like he'd soiled his pants and when he flagged down the bus his arms flailed like a marionette. The topic of aquatic life was the only thing that could arouse Forest from an otherwise constant look of bewilderment.

Celia, Forest and the sacred fetus made an amazingly easy transition to Gainesville, Florida where Forest studied marine biology. Celia who had skittered through life like a spooked colt added keys and a name tag to her scapular as assistant manager of Walmart's Junior Fashions at the Sunshine Mall. Their daughter Cyndi was a sterling example of genetic vagary. Or perhaps it is all in the name. They named their daughter something that would bring levity into their lives. Cyndi lived up to it. She was spared Celia's frailty and Forest's looks and along with a Tiffany, two Bambi's and a few Ambers won several Little Sunshine beauty pageants.

Upon graduation Forest moved his little family further south to Davie, Florida. Celia continued traipsing through the aisles of Walmart straightening end caps and talking officiously over her Walkie Talkie. Now her wardrobe consisted of knits from the "Ladies on the Go" department. The Peter Pan blouses and plaid skirts had been tossed in a Goodwill box on Dixie Highway.

One February after visiting her sister, Missy was overcome with dread at the idea of returning to her solitary existence in Rogers Park. She decided on the plane that hearing about Walmart's theft prevention and a manatees' genitals were preferable to another breakfast alone at Cullen's on Devon Avenue. The following April Missy was unpacking margarita glasses etched with palm trees at Hibiscus Hamlet. It was through default that Missy ended up at the 'Hamlet.' She had envisioned herself nearer the ocean in one of the dissolute sultry little bungalows hidden behind entanglements of wanton growth. Most of those places had roaches with squatter's rights and no central air. But in spite of this and occasional reports of sliced up torsos scattered among the foliage, they were expensive. Missy would eventually uncover the reasons for South Florida's enigmatic behavior. Romantic notions factor big into reckless spending. The sun and ocean hold the promise of a succulent and carefree life as well as impunity from winter melancholy for the emotionally anemic like Missy.

Cyndi was fifteen when Celia began to use oblique terms like "a little dickens" or "a handful" when talking about her only child. One evening when Missy had just settled in with a drink and her Wheel of Fortune Cyndi appeared at the door with a small white garbage bag and a sheepish smile. She held a note from Celia "Do you want a roommate for the weekend?" The next day Missy took her niece to the mall. Cyndi trailed behind her with the expression of someone who was being abducted by a religious cult. Missy purchased a lot of ruffles and satin for the guest room and in return she acquired a regular weekend companion to the Miami ballet in Coral Gables.

Cyndi's departure was as unexpected as her arrival. She left quietly one Friday night to the sound of a horn accompanied once again by a garbage bag. The car belonged Raymond who, with his pinched face and spiked hair, resembled a bustard. He was arrested a week later for robbing a Publix Food Store in Fort Lauderdale leaving Cyndi with child. Missy's sudden lack of a weekend roommate was the least of her disappointment. Like bad perms she thought these kind of calamities were passé'. Things were supposed to be easier for Cyndi's generation. The world had not been Missy's oyster at eighteen. It was a terrain of land mines on which women tread cautiously. The world in her day was a world of danger, of "what ifs" at every turn. The only escape from the male brute was to marry one; a choice Missy never had the luxury of making. She had worked close to home at St Gertrude's rectory until a new priest arrived with his mother, Bernice, who replaced her. Missy was stunned by the loss of her job and preferring to stay in the neighborhood spent the rest of her working life as a shampoo girl at Mitzi's on Ashland Ave, a block from her home.

Even before her daughter was born Cyndi found a "soul mate" in Casey. From what Missy could determine their spiritual bond was Miller Lite and the Cove on Dania Beach. The couple had met there and had their wedding ceremony there. Besides the

Cove their social life was Sunshine Mall. Casey would happily follow behind Cyndi lumbering past the kiosks his palms facing back like a primate always on the lookout for a cute butt and warm pretzel. Missy wondered if they had named the new baby Annie after a saint or a pretzel. In addition to discussing Casey's preternatural laziness Cyndi talked incessantly about this seemingly ordinary petulant child in empyrean terms implying that she was the wunderkind of South Broward's school system.

And on this particular Tuesday afternoon Missy desperately wanted to be alone and ruminate over her finances when she heard "Hey, girlfriend!!"

"My god! My favorite girls! What brings you to the mall?" Missy forced a grin.

She figured it was another clothing return which was Cyndi's favorite pastime. She wasn't averse to wearing a garment and bringing it back. Today it was a puffy hemline.

"Can Annie come home with you, Auntie Margaret? I was going to call you but hell, here you are in the flesh."

"Sure. How long are you going to be gone?"

"Not long. You gals can bond or whatever."

Missy turned to Annie. " You can help me pick out some normal clothes. Pretend you're that girl on that TV show 'What Not to Wear.'"

Annie looked at her with horror. She waved at her mom like she was being led to her execution.

"Oh what fun, just you and me!" Missy was trying be like the zany great aunt out of a television sitcom but when she gazed at the sparkling orange a few feet ahead of her she again muttered "Mother would die."

"We'll stop on the way home and get some corn dogs and root beer. That was your mom's favorite."

"I don't eat that stuff; only organic fruit and vegetables from Whole Foods. Maybe I can do chicken tacos and an Evian water if you're going to YOUR grocery store." She was engrossed in texting. Her purple nails were working at such a frantic pace Missy wondered if she was devising an escape plan.

Back at the Hamlet they watched a reality show that involved a lot of screaming among several anorexic looking women. Annie left the room and didn't came back. Missy discovered her asleep in a pair of her mom's old sweat pants hugging her cell phone. She felt compelled to wake her.

"Are you ok? Don't you ever eat?"

"I'm tired. Wake me when mom comes." Then a barely audible "Love you, Aunt Margaret."

Missy ended the day as she started it, staring into space. Only now she was listening to Bach and sipping a martini and feeling more benevolent by the moment.

Her reverie was broken by the sound of Carrie Underwood blasting from a car and Cyndi looking all hyped up carrying a letter and a duffle bag. The oaf was following behind. They had matching flip flops and goofy expressions.

"God, they robbed a bank." Missy felt faint. She had an image of her mother saying the Rosary.

"Where is my baby?" Cyndi's giggling frightened Missy.

Just then Annie appeared at the bedroom doorway with smeared mascara and a snarl.

"Put your shoes on, Pookie. We're taking you to Red Lobster." Just then Missy heard rustling and whimpering in the duffle bag. The two women were gushing over a very small dog. The barking and stench of dog urine was making Missy queasy.

"Can you beat this?"

She handed a letter to Missy. At first she skimmed it thinking it was some kind of bull-shit scam like a "free" trip to Las Vegas. But at second glance it appeared to be a scholarship to the New York School of Ballet. Yes. It was a letter for Annie, a dazzling letter.

"I'm speechless." Missy felt like she did at Christmas Mass when the choir was singing. She hugged them all including the new puppy and Casey.

"See, Aunt Margaret, remember all those ballets we attended? Well my girl here inherited your love for that stuff."

Annie threw her great aunt a kiss as she ran to car.

"I love Bach too, Aunt Margaret."

"Call me Aunt Missy!" she yelled out the door and sat back down on her new sofa with one more cocktail.

CHAPTER 2

Hunted

I'll begin by telling the reader it was a Monday. I know this for certain because on Mondays I go into Evanston, a half hour bus ride from my apartment in Chicago. Often I will meet Francis for a Starbucks and then both of us will proceed to the library's weekly book sale. I always feel as though I have to qualify my relationship with Francis. He's my 'ex' but I find that term as well as the whole divorce thing vulgar. So for all practical purposes not too much has changed except separate homes and even less money. Our Mondays are the only social commitment I can abide. Even something as innocuous as an evening movie date hits me with the languor of a tropical disease.

This particular Monday held the usual capricious Chicago weather. It was late May but cold and gray. Of course those snotty rich Northwestern students who could clothe a third world country were walking around in torn cargo shorts and ragged t shirts. Francis is always late and I waited inside Starbucks for him. I felt like a spectacle in my hunter's cap and puffy jacket.

I love my city and try not to whine about its weather. Hearing Francis tell people he loves Chicago and embraces its cultural charm makes me slightly bilious. Embracing means loving unconditionally the slush, green pigeon slime and crazies on the el train. Francis 'embraces' from a Metra train on his way in from the suburbs while I, on the other hand, am one of the huddled masses wedged between a sari that reeks of garlic and a creature with a cart filled with all his worldly possessions muttering to the diesel fumes on the Clark Street bus. I wait on benches next to stoic old men built like eroded granite who give me the eye and toothless old ladies in knee highs who grumble in foreign languages.

Back to my story. After our usual black coffee we walk the block to the library. On Mondays they put the new donations in an alcove next to periodicals. Francis meanders while I continue my quest for a pristine first edition. A woman next to me was man-handling the books in a way that suggests quick resale on e-bay which I consider sacrilegious. Sensing my agitation she introduced herself. Misty had the sad glamour of the dollar store's rendition of a Barbie doll. She was stick thin and plastered with makeup. Her eyes were frightfully large with a stunned imploring expression. But even an addled brain an sense scorn. She gave me a creepy quivering half smile.

"I'm matching dust covers with my new furniture." she offered.

I mentioned this later to Francis and suggested she might have a major thyroid problem. "Mimi, she's off her nut. I could hear her all the way back in Mysteries."

When I left the job scene or rather when the recession parted us I interviewed for jobs that only the elderly and refugees would consider. I proceeded to prostrate myself at the feet of a few men whom, under any other circumstance, I would have avoided. I did a lot of silly blathering when interviewed by a woman who smelled like licorice and cat food and whose office was decorated with pictures of Tweety Bird. One morning around four a.m., when I get my epiphanies, I realized I'd rather be broke then report to a Dave or a Holly. I resorted to reading self-help books whose common thread was to pursue your passion and happiness would follow. Writing is my passion but it is a solitary trade. Book collecting, another interest, seems to attract hoarders, cat people and people that harbor conspiracy theories. So I have to admit Misty's timing was perfect. At another time those haunted eyes would have been a deterrent. Even her name was atypical of the bibliophile circuit. Pole dancers have names like Misty. Names like that are untrustworthy. But Misty was full of shtick; another Joan Rivers. In the length of time I had secured a Faulkner in mint condition she had handed me her business card and in a hoarse but chipper voice rattled off her life. I caught something about investments and rehabbing a two flat in Uptown. I didn't remember much. For all that talk she still lacked identity. Her bony bluish hands were fluttering like a feather and she used a lot of hackneyed phrases to round things off like "If You Will" and "God help me." She said "At the end of the day" twice in one breath. She was dancing to her voice. Her three inch heels were hopping from one foot to the other. She wore a turquoise wraparound dress that could have been a Von Furstenberg but it was a little too imposing for a morning at the library and on her emaciated body it looked more like a shroud. She had turquoise accessories as well; chunky Southwestern stuff I see on those home shopping shows for the "fashion conscious." But hell I wanted a friend, whirling dervish or not. I do recall something about her becoming a healed spirit from a meditation retreat where she was encircled by doves. Yes, doves. But if she drank I would keep her.

When she called the following week I accepted a date for a cocktail at O'Grady's pub in Evanston. She insisted on sitting outside where she could "hear herself talk". It was chilly but Northwestern students were drinking up a storm in t-shirts and flip flops. I counted the word "awesome "16 times and some dog tried to sniff my crotch. There were bikes, kids, music and the drinks were twelve dollars. It was a fucking expensive Calcutta. As Francis would later say "No one twisted your arm, Mimi" but somehow while I was pondering the bill and a child standing on a table she finagled another date.

By Thursday of the following week I was feeling wretched; overcome by a paralyzing torpor. I was sure it was some type of rare blood disease but I was afraid to cancel. I knew instinctively she had the makings of a madman and I felt too sick to handle unhinged recriminations. I lay in bed picturing my memorial service. People referring to me as zany; or worse a "friendly soul who befriended everyone she met." Would Francis remember to play Bach's cantata 140?

We met at a café on Clark and to my chagrin it was b.y.o.b. Misty however had known and brought two bottles of red wine which makes me wheeze. The theme of her conversation that night was metaphysical; a coinciding of planets and events in

Misty Bordeaux's important existence. I was too enmeshed in daydreaming about a martini to focus on her theories. Yes, she was off the beam. Nevertheless I let her drunken ass weave her Ford Focus down Clark street to my apartment. She hinted at coming up but I told her my aged mother was sleeping. My mother is buried at Hibiscus Haven cemetery in Boca Raton, Fla.

I couldn't sleep that night. Ideas of restraining orders and witness protection programs kept me awake. I pictured myself living anonymously in a trailer park in Ocala, Florida with a guard dog.

I called Francis. "Protect me."

He laughed "From what?"

"From me. I wish I had never connected with this broad."

"Wish in one hand and shit in the other. See which fills up faster." Francis uses this saying at any possible opportunity.

I woke at dawn with a literal shit fit. I had a clinically profound hangover from that godawful wine with its accompanying anxiety. I was on the toilet when she called. Due to my hyper vigilant state my cell phone was on my lap.

"Mimi, forgive me for talking so much last night. Let me make it up to you. Didn't you tell me you liked an author named Hemon? Well he's giving a reading at the downtown library."

I called my sister Sheila. "God Almighty! Only you could meet a Misty at a library. I thought Mistys gave lap dances."

"I'll give her one more chance. She's driving me to see my favorite writer, Aleksandar Hemon, at the Chicago Public Library. She'll be too awed by whom she calls the 'intellectuals' to misbehave."

"Maybe you should revisit the idea of coming to Florida. I did the guest bedroom in shabby chic. Oh, and trust me, she will misbehave."

"I can't listen to those fuzzy headed broads talk about food and diets. But thanks. I'll keep it in mind."

Incredibly she did misbehave. Question/answer time is sort of a formality and any questions are usually intelligent and concise. Hemon looked sick and anyone with an ounce of sensitivity would have known that. Misty stood up and it was obvious she was composing something as she grabbed the microphone. She was doing something with her mouth that was slappable.

"Mr Hemon, how do you like our fair city?"

Hemon looked like he wanted to choke the anorexic morsel of a creature. I walked ahead of her into the lobby but of course, she had to scream at no one in particular.

"Oh Jesus! Twenty five dollars for a book! That's two cocktails."

I desperately wanted my bed but she was my ride and she wanted a "night cap."

"That's why women don't go far in life`." She paused. I waited. She did hat thing with her mouth again.

"They are afraid to show their intelligence. Notice I was the only women to talk except for that little Asian and what the hell does 'conceit' have to do with writing?"

The evening ended on a down note. Misty's face had become bloated and her eyes puffy. She suddenly gave me a litany of abuse she'd sustained over her lifetime including more than one financial fleecing. I kept thinking of my bed and my cat, Mo, and wondering why Misty and not I had some kind of gainful employment. Suddenly she stopped talking and stared at me in that fixated way of hers. This lasted for so long I thought she was having a seizure. She was even drooling a little.

"Mimi, you have some spinach dip in your front teeth."

I hailed a taxi and immediately called Francis when I returned home.

"She's a moron and a crazy one."

Several weeks had passed so I didn't hesitate to pick up my phone one evening during Wheel of Fortune. The voice on the other end was so hoarse it didn't register right away.

"This is Misty. You've probably wondered where I've been." I was too shocked to respond.

"Well, breathe easy my friend."

I was having a mild panic attack and at the same time wondering if Francis could buy me a ticket to Florida. More silence. "I'm back on the scene." Silence again. Then in the nasally voice of one who's been drinking, "I'm too god damn nice. I've had time to reflect and now it's so clear. I have been too nice all my life. But I'm a survivor. Look, I know my baggage may be too much for some people but an old friend is in town and he's got loads of charisma. Trust me you'll love him!"

Now this is where my sanity has to be questioned. I agreed to meet Gary Zink.

"You won't regret this, Mimi. Gary helped me through a few crises and he can help you."

I didn't think I was in the throes of a crisis but apparently suicidal is among the qualities Misty looks for in a friend. His name brought to mind a face on a billboard with the caption 'Call Gary Zink your personal injury attorney.'

We met on Belmont Avenue at PJ Clarke's and unfortunately I was prophetic. He had the facial expression of a paper doll. His eyes were tiny and unfocused. This was not a man I could imagine as a callow child. This was a face that had an 800 number underneath it; a species that germinates in dark airport hotel bars at night like a vampire and in the morning taps a microphone in some catacomb of a meeting room. To a segment of society he is their savior; the man with the secret formula. He attracts that smug, greedy individual who will drive long distances to sit in a folding chair, eat a donut hole and drool over outlandish schemes.

At the end of the night I still hadn't figured out Gary's deal but I did know he wrote about it. Following a gusty swallow of his Manhattan he told me he had finished a great book on the plane. Foolish me. I straightened up and asked who wrote it. Another swallow and he answered with a snort, "Me. Who else?" He grabbed a copy from his briefcase.

"Pay me when you make your first million. Anyone looking to have the American dream needs this. For a measly twenty two dollars you can get out of the dregs and own a slice of life." He raised his glass and with a smarmy grin exposed a missing tooth.

This was the end. I did not buy his book. I did not answer Misty's slurred questions pertaining to my own self-realization. I took a bus home and by midnight I had purchased a ticket to Florida. When I returned a week later her calls had stopped. I felt like I'd been delivered from some horrific hostage situation whose true vileness is only fully realized in hindsight.

Eventually I resumed my old schedule without a vision of Misty looming in the corner of my brain. I was giddy the first time

I ventured back into Evanston. Sitting in Nevins's Pub that first evening was heaven except instead of listening to Francis I kept looking around for Misty. Her absence was unnerving. Francis was in the bathroom when two clammy hands blinded me.

"Guess who." in that same scratchy voice. "Can I join you?"

Francis graciously took her bony bluish hand "Misty. Am I right?"

"You bet." She replied." Can we have a cocktail in a quiet corner." We followed her into a corner booth.

"I'm not going to spoil your evening but I just needed a friend and drinks are on me."

Damn, I can never refuse a little drink with a little drama. Her eyes were glistening. The mouth twitched.

"My used-to-be friend, Gary, took me for big mullah. He's nowhere to be found and I'm living out of my car."

I knew she wanted to pursue this delectably tragic story but my survival skills took over. I told her I had to go visit my mother who was at death's door. Francis stopped at my place for a night-cap. I started crying.

"I'm fucked. She's on my trail and desperate."

Misty seemed too fragile to hunt me down but I watch too many true crime shows and wasn't totally convinced. The dames who load twenty shots into their sleeping spouses are thin lipped, petite blonds with that same wild eyed expression. I wasn't comfortable sticking around my apartment. While sipping morning coffee I would choreograph my travels. I searched out a newly opened used bookstore in a sketchy neighborhood that required a train and two buses. I wore a drab 'don't fuck with me' outfit and a fanny pack hidden under my jacket. Chicago can turn on you fast. The following week I stayed nearer my turf spending an afternoon on Lincoln Avenue where I fondled forty dollar candles because they were made by local "artisans". I spent a month on these odd excursions feeling out of kilter and, to quote Francis, "chomping at the bit" to go back to Evanston.

One sunny Monday I decided that this would be a good morning to try out my new red shopping cart, a gift from Francis. They're back in style thanks to Ikea. On the way home from the grocery store I saw what appeared to be a giant red ball on my front stoop. As I approached, the ball slowly unraveled into a red nylon jogging suit. Misty stood up at attention like she was in drill practice.

"I've been waiting here an hour. I thought you were not answering the bell. I only wanted to apologize for me just being me. I'm a pain in the ass. I know that but I haven't had it easy you know. My mother never wanted me. Anyway I would be honored to take you to dinner tonight.

"Not a chance. I have to write. Nothing personal but I can't drink and write."

With that, and I know this sounds unbelievable, she took a pistol from her purse. I'd never seen one in real life. With her free hand she dumped library books from a satchel. First she aimed at me then turned the gun on herself, pointing it at her concave chest. Then as I'm squinting and trying to recall the Act of Contrition she turned the pistol towards the books. There were five shots in all. I don't remember the cops or the neighbors' comforting gestures. But I do remember taking note of the books. One had to do with money ;the other on making friends. The whole thing had me baffled but when you think about it I guess it all makes sense.

CHAPTER 3

Centrally Located

People who knew him could accurately describe Edmund as a creature of habit. He had been divorced for many years and lived with his mother, Agnes. He liked to think of it more a bachelor pad with a housekeeper who cooked his meals and pressed his underwear. Edmund did the storm windows, the yard and occasionally the yard of their neighbor, an acerbic French woman who did not suffer old age gladly. Claudette had bold black eyebrows aggressively drawn to the ridge of her nose and uneven streaks of eye shadow underneath a wig of auburn poodle curls. She would pace around her little house smoking Cigarillos from of her smudged cranberry lips while inventing more tasks for Edmund. Her raspy voice issuing orders out of different windows splintered the sounds of robins and his daydreams of winning big in the Illinois lottery.

His breakfast seldom deviated from freshly squeezed orange juice, coffee and cereal with raisin bread toast served separately on a smaller porcelain plate. When he finished he would return to his bedroom in a very roughly converted basement to check his email and watch the news while he waited to "move his bowels". Other predictable events played into his daily schedule. Almost every morning he went "uptown" to Quick Mart saying the same thing when he left the house.He would wait until he was out the door and shout "Off to the races" hoping if he was fast enough Agnes wouldn't drum up something she needed at the grocery store. As he was always watching his money the rest of his day presented monotonous choices. He would alternate between the library, lunch with his ex-wife Grace or taking Agnes on errands. Walking up the slight incline he looked like a man on a mission with his legs slightly bent and his head stretched forward as if he was catching a strange scent. But Ahmar and Lamar knew better. He required just a few tickets, a pack of Marlborough's, some sports talk and he was out the door and back down Chestnut Hill. At least once a month he met his ex-wife for lunch in Evanston, a halfway mark for both. They'd ironed out old differences by simply focusing on new ones. She'd do most of the talking as he chomped furiously, his large waxy ears moving in cadence with his mouth. Every so often he would stop to examine his food and nod to Grace. They had three things in common: a daughter, a granddaughter and an alarming lack of funds.

The two had met at Butch McGuire's bar on Division Street. In those days a girl didn't linger too long downtown. They "got" the guy and got out of there. For girls of proper Irish Catholic breeding dating was a brief chapter, just enough to provide antidotes for their wedding reception and progeny.Within six months after sitting on bar stools they were enmeshed in guest lists and caterers. Grace had let her Sassoon hair cut grow out so that her veil covered the chaste chin length bob of her parochial school days. Two years later things had gone from festive to grim. Edmund was overwhelmed by parenthood and bills. Anything domestic had become his Stations of the Cross. His friends were still at Butch McGuire's on Friday nights while he was trapped in a small apartment that smelled like sour milk and Lysol. He began to consider Grace his saboteur.

His job paid a decent income but hardly enough for three. He worked in a market research firm which didn't have quite the élan of the Leo Burnett Advertising Agency where some of his pals were working. Instead of the tony Gold Coast he was commuting to a small family owned business in a cement building west of the loop under an el track. He ate lunch in the cafeteria because the neighborhood was a stark grey wasteland.Beer cans. whisky bottles and drunks were pugnaciously strewn in his path and paper floated about like tumbleweed. Except for a statue of Mary peering out from a windowsill or a bike lying in a gangway the neighborhood looked abandoned. One winter morning a toothless man in flip flops, cargo shorts and a torn Cubs shirt followed him from the bus. Edmund was more ashamed than afraid. That he was subject to this kind of indignity as well as a colicky baby and bank overdrafts made him weep.He felt like he did as an altar boy when he wet his pants coming home from St Michael's one brutally cold morning. He could barely work the rest of the day. He needed someone to bolster his ego. Several times that day he had to refrain from calling his mom. That night he met a few friends on Division Street and returned to Evanston sullen and sloppy at dawn. What he really wanted eluded him.

Images came to him only after a few drinks. They included pithy ad slogans with him in a Brooks Brothers suit surrounded by long legged red headed women. But his ideas were fragile and he lost track of them going to the men's room.

Change usually comes in merciful increments. This was the case with Edmund and his mom who had enjoyed a mostly sanguine existence until the winter Agnes started burning things. At first it was hard boiled eggs popping in the saucepan which she mistook for gunshots in her backyard. "Everyone burns eggs" assured his sister, Mary Pat. When she was spotted walking to Mass in her slip Edmund knew the jig was up. The house would have to be sold and his life 'on easy street' as his sister described it, was over. Mother would go to Spring Haven Assisted Living in Northbrook. The move evolved into contretemps and late night phone calls with wailing and retributions. He had been almost afraid to tell Grace and his daughter Anna whom he had helped throughout the years. "What a mess" he would repeat over and over as we walked uptown for his lottery tickets. Sometimes he felt like he was at Camp David with all the discussion. He called his sister, Mary Pat.

"Listen I need some money for my transition. You know, just to square things."

"What the hell does that mean? You've been transitioning for twenty years at Moms. I need holistic treatment for my back and my insurance doesn't pay for it. If it doesn't work then it's a plane ticket to Our Lady of Medjugorje."

Packing up the house presented its own unique agony. His mother insisted on taking boxes of old pictures, school artwork and her many crucifixes'. Stripped of her duties she seemed to

Edmund both wanton and fragile which elicited a combination of fear and sadness. At night when Edmund got up to have a cigarette he would see an unsettling apparition in the blue house-coat decorated in parrots and palm trees that Mary Pat had given to her one Christmas. She was an old lady, a stooped banshee roaming the house at odd hours straightening doilies and studying her hands. Mary Pat came over frequently to oversee the packing and sale of the house. She loved throwing out real estate jargon along with the ceramic vases. Suddenly her back seemed cured. She'd be at the kitchen table with her glasses on the tip her nose jotting notes or outside talking officiously to any neighbor she could corner. Edmund had assured himself that an old dank house with loose baseboards and an outdated kitchen would not sell. But within two months of planting the 'For Sale' sign next to the petunia bed Lamar's son and daughter-in- law were calling it home.

The conversations over his mother's welfare and apartment hunting increased his smoking and exhausted him. He followed ads in the North Shore Review and looked at a third floor in a converted house in Evanston next door to the courtyard apartment building he and Grace had lived when they were married. As a married couple they had given the appearance of prosperity with furniture from John M Smythe, dried flowers from Old Town, cocktail table books from Kroch's and Brentano's and Peter Max towels from Crate and Barrel.

Grace was calling at obscene hours and Edmund was sure he detected a slur in her speech. She'd start by asking pleasantries about his mom and his apartment search and suddenly veer into volcanic outbursts. "Pray I keep the wolves at the door" or "You know you could get a part time job and save me from sleepless nights." Edmund couldn't think about the wolves. He needed all his money and he'd be "God Damned" if he'd be forced into some disgraceful job like a senior greeter at Wal Mart. He remembered with cold terror Wally Wiggins the crossing guard at his grade school. The old man made sure everyone knew that as a shoe salesman he had won several trips to Hawaii.But in the end Wally was just a crossing guard who told corny jokes. Edmund was offended by Grace's insensitivity during such a trying time but nevertheless guilt still niggled at him. Was she really afraid she'd end up sleeping in the Metra train station or was that a sympathy ploy? He decided that the longer you know a person the more confusing they become. This person screaming over the phone was not the gentle woman who nightly served him a three course dinner dutifully remembering to serve the salad on a separate plate. She had never complained that changing babies made him dry heave. He had been under the delusion that she understood his need to 'unwind' with the guys and come back to an immaculate home. Once as newlyweds Agnes had come for coffee saying she wanted "girl time" with Grace but then pursed her lips and pulled an apron from her bag.She had proceeded to present her daughter-in-law with Murphy soap and a package of sponges as if they were family heirlooms. She stressed the need for cleaning the walls twice a year as Edmund was allergic to dust. She reminded Grace that cat hair was a threat to everyone's health and Ivory Flakes were the gentlest on clothes. As she was leaving she deposited a list of Edmunds favorite meals on the kitchen counter.

Edmund like to say that he loved the vitality of the city but anything past its northernmost borderline of Howard Street made him nervous. He didn't mind "minorities" just "not in packs." The third floor of the frame house on Forest Ave had become increasingly attractive. The idea of living in a converted attic was demoralizing but it was affordable and like Mary Pat reminded him daily it was all about location. He put the walnut tea cart in the foyer. He installed the imperious "divan" with its imbedded ketchup crust and Agnes' tales of doom along with its matching floral recliner around the claw legged coffee table. After unpacking and placing a few of Agnes' LLadros on the walnut side table he reluctantly notified the post office of his new home. Once a week he would half-heartedly look for a part time job in the neighborhood but mostly he pondered his state of affairs over coffee and cigarettes. He secretly missed Agnes pushing the Hoover under his feet while reminding him of the latest deaths in the parish. Just the thought of maneuvering around grocery stores and doing laundry was daunting. His mother had known the exact ratio of ingredients for his oatmeal and the recipe for his chocolate chip cookies and apple strudel. He couldn't imagine a winter meal without her stewed prunes and homemade applesauce. Just thinking of it made him sigh deeply and often and stare out the kitchen window in an almost catatonic state.

Agnes was finally ensconced in quarters no bigger than her previous living room. Edmund was appalled by the volume of geriatric atrocities and the desperate attempts at cheeriness in spite of a subtle but constant aroma of urine that persisted throughout the corridors. But his mother was astonishingly content. Her conversations were filled with gleeful gossip and boisterous complaints. In fact not long after Edmund would arrive following an hour trip on two buses she would become antsy.

"Darling, I have to go to the bathroom " or "naptime for the old girl" and she'd look at him peevishly like he was a pesky stray.

Edmund was becoming somewhat acclimated to his own place. His living room faced Forest Ave and an apple tree. A grammar school was across the street and Edmund found the childish sounds uplifting. The kitchen was ample enough for someone who opened cans. The bedroom was small but he had little furniture. He still slept in the maple twin bed of his childhood under the same chenille bedspread. There was an enclosed porch off the kitchen where he smoked and ruminated over things. But Edmund wasn't given to unequivocal contentment. Over lunch one Friday he complained to Grace "I've seen both men and women with long grey hair and beads looking like they're at Woodstock. There are too many health food stores and no grocery stores for the regular guy. And I can't find a simple cheap coffee shop. They're all called cafes. I went all over town trying to buy a pair of socks last week. I passed a candle shop and a place for dog massages but no socks. I'm in a fucking commune with a bunch of left wing fruitcakes. Where am I?"

By the beginning of the second week after the last box had been emptied and the cable guy had left following several hours of reassuring banter Edmund began to have some unsettling thoughts. He always awoke at five for his first cigarette while indulging in his usual chimera of a lottery win or kicking his smoking habit and becoming a bodybuilder. But lately a pall cloaked the still surroundings. From the back porch he could see the bedroom where Anna was conceived. At first he construed this as a good sign but it was becoming increasingly ominous. At the onset of day Edmund would linger in bed, one hand under the flat feather pillow and the other nestled between his thighs, besieged by sadness.

When they divorced Grace spewed so many accusations and retributions Edmund couldn't absorb them all at once. Nor did he want to. Alcohol seemed to temporarily buffer the anguish. But after his second DUI he quit drinking and for months he could only concentrate on the simplest of tasks. He would half listen to his mother's daily reports on both local and global tragedies and her litany of house repairs. "I have a feeling the roof is leaking because I see water in strange places. or "I think there's mold in the basement. I feel light headed down there." "That toilet keeps gurgling; probably costing a mint in water bills." Edmund would just nod and perhaps jot something down as if he were going to run to Home Depot. But with his sobriety this kind of chatter became unnerving. He felt like he had some exotic illness that required sterile and gentle handling.

Now unpleasant memories were lurking in his frontal cortex like an awning that could at any second give way to rain. His old parking space in back reminded him of a grave site.After their divorce Grace had tearfully recalled the many nights she waited for the rumbling of the Pinto as it pulled up in the alley. Edmund could no longer enjoy a cigarette on his back porch. He started walking the two blocks to Lake Michigan but that was tiresome and irritating. He was sure that smokers were tantamount to pedophiles in Evanston. Evanston people were particularly big on health and clean air. He did the only sensible thing. He bought a nicotine patch and quit smoking. This was torturous for someone who had carried Marlboros in his pocket for almost fifty years. He could not avoid the parking spot when he emptied the garbage and the memories begin to plague him throughout the day. He bought an IPod thinking music might distill his thoughts. He played Miles Davis' At the Savoy and Nina Simone when he puttered around the apartment. It didn't work. The songs reminded him of the times he was drunk and how the loud music would wake Anna.He began staying out as long as possible. The people he had ridiculed who hung out for hours at a bookstore cafe were now his comrades and the store his fortress. He had begun to look forward to the company of a few retirees. Exchanging amiable words made him feel like a decent human. A menacing aura that would later follow him up the three flights of stairs made him briefly consider a dog. Later on however wrapped snuggly in his terry cloth robe watching Jeopardy and eating Kraft Macaroni and Cheese he changed his mind. Dogs were too much money, work and worry, especially worry. He liked to think of himself as a "man on the go "without responsibilities."

One day he was unable to go to a bookstore. He was in fact unable to get off the couch. He could not decide if this was a general malaise or the flu. He lay perfectly still staring at a spider dangling from the brass lion on the Stiffel lamp. He applied a damp washcloth to his forehead like his mother would have done. PBS was featuring old TV shows. Arthur Godfrey was cracking some stale jokes and playing a ukulele. The voice triggered sublime moments of childhood, eating peanut butter sandwiches and drinking Bosco while Agnes pressed sheets in her mangle. Later that night Edmund is suddenly sitting upright on the edge of his bed, His alertness baffles him. He is sure it has nothing to do with the bankruptcy lawyer promising a new lease on life or the blond selling something called a Tummy Tucker on the TV. A noise from the alley makes him stiffen. A woman screams "Stop Carl" followed by loud weeping. He grabs the hammer he kept on the night table by his Rosary and runs down the back stairs infused with invincibility. He hears another voice; the voice of a younger passionate Edmund.

Later he could describe it as blind rage. He felt fierce like Max in Anna's favorite childhood book Where the Wild Things Are who was undaunted by the monsters. A young Hispanic woman was up against a car and a squat burly guy was slapping her.

"Stop you son of a bitch." Edmund was sobbing and yelling. And all of his one hundred and forty pound body was lunging at this torso of tattooed flesh that he described later as a tree trunk. The girl was crouched down against the car with her arms folded against her chest. The man looked at Edmund "Fuck you man.You don't get it! She fucked with me and that don't work where I come from". Edmund's bravado was enhanced when he noticed that the guy had placed his hand on the car for support. He began hopping from one foot to the other swinging the hammer in the air while the man turned and wobbled away. Edmund found the strength to lift the girl up to a standing position and hug her. Someone had already called 911. After he finished with the police paperwork he gave Amelia his name and number assuring her of future protection. As he walked upstairs his body rumbled and gurgled like the old Pinto finally coming to rest.

The next morning was chilly and cloudy. A few raindrops hit his kitchen window as he squeezed juice. Yes, Edmund was squeezing juice from oranges he had purchased weeks ago. There were eggs in the new frying pan and he was singing an old Nina Simone tune. Outside the world was more vivid; the sky was a childlike blue and the sun was a crayon yellow. Edmund now felt competent enough for a little "time filler job" and hell maybe a dog. It would be a good opener with women at the dog park. He thought about a dog. a job and a woman.

"I'll never get any dog of mine a massage" he thought. With that he kicked a few stones up to the heavens and did something he'd never done before. He thanked a God of clarity and order who leaves nothing to chance.

CHAPTER 4

Maxed Out

I am of that generation whose shopping annals include the dawn of malls and the credit cards that infused them with life.

I was born in Rogers Park on Chicago's Northside where all needs were met within a mile of our apartment. Winsbergs Department Store accommodated us with shoes, school uniforms and hair permanents. Woolworths provided the odds and ends. My mother's weekly shopping at the A&P commenced at our oil cloth covered kitchen table where she arranged her coffee, a small sponge, and a jelly jar of water. With the steely glint of someone who is in imminent possession of another baby blue bath towel she would studiously paste her S & H green stamps in a booklet.

Twice a year we ventured out of our neighborhood and into the "loop." If it was Christmas we would go for the windows and Santa and in the Spring for Marshal Field's annual white sale. Shopping was a rapid stern affair allowing for only a sliver of levity with new paper dolls. Life was simple. It was restrained and tailored with uncluttered closets. All of my toys fit nicely into a small foot locker which fit nicely under the window in the dining room.

With the advent of malls and credit cards all hell broke loose. Shopping was no longer a task but a hobby with festive bumper stickers like "shop till you drop" on the back of a Volkswagen. When I was ten my father had a heart attack and my parents made a stunning transition from Chicago to South East Florida. It was here that I had my first mall experience. The Sears Mall was located about two miles west of our little yellow stucco house in Hollywood. The bright lights, sweet errant aroma of sweat, popcorn and fruit drinks called Mango Delight were the stuff of fairy tales. To use my favorite word at that time shopping was a "blast." It was a virtual bacchanal with Sears at one end and Burdines at the other and my mother's MasterCard the master of ceremonies. This kind of frivolity called for a different look; a pastel pants suit and a bouffant replaced the hat and gloves and cropped curls.

Our shopping day began with mom in her underwear and too much Friendship Gardens sitting at her bedroom window with a magnifying mirror, applying makeup or as she would say "putting on her face;" starting with Maybelline cake mascara in a red box and ending with a grand sweep of Coty face powder and an application of lipstick too pink and blunt so that a bright smudge bridged her cupid's bow. But I would never dare tell her. Daughters didn't do that kind of thing. Before she chose the clip-on earrings she would take her straw purse down from the closet shelf, stuff it with her Chiclets gum, Kleenex, car keys and the magic CARD. She never got the hang of the stick shift so we would more or less lurch down Hollywood Blvd towards the Holy Grail. Mom's presence played an essential part in these outings and not for the obvious reasons of car and credit card but for her steady solid sweet company. We never indulged in soul searching conversations but those no nonsense, purposeful strides through the aisles searching for my clothes while reminding me about my high waist and long butt were somehow comforting.

I moved back to Chicago after college but visited at least once a year. My first two children were sixteen months apart and she used the Sear Revolving Card to buy me a double stroller. On that same day she charged a pair of hounds tooth bell bottoms for my husband, Patrick, leading to my theory that the combo of heat and credit deprives the brain of oxygen. I remember the store was called Just Pants and the clerk was a snide patronizing brat. Mom was giddy over her uncharacteristically whimsical purchase and I was sad over that fact that she mistakenly believed Patrick was resilient enough to wear those bell bottoms and that unbeknown to her we were going through the brambles and thorns of a young marriage. I was wrong on the first and right on the second.

When my kids were older, mom and I resumed our solo shopping trips. By now we had advanced beyond the honkytonk playground of Sears Mall and were traversing the fountains and corridors of Galleria and Ventura. Sometimes she'd sit it out with the excuse of people watching while I perused the stores. Occasionally I'd pass her unexpectedly and be startled by her frailty. Considering todays life span she was only middle old at the time, a mere eighty, and I didn't like to see her losing her edge. I wanted her to follow me around reminding me that that

I'm such an attractive girl but I have to buy clothes suited for my body type. As soon as we got home she'd toss her bra, put on a shift and replace her credit card in the desk. Then she'd unfold a plastic webbed beach chair and fold laundry while drinking her 90 proof Old Granddad and listening to me and what now seems an incorrigible litany of self-centered tripe. I imagine that to this very literal, emotionally substantial Nebraska farm gal I must have seemed mildly unhinged.

My children have grown. I now have my first grandchild. After much grave deliberation my older sister, Mary has placed mom in a nursing home. My first sight of her in such a sad powerless state was unbearable and I had to leave. Mary told me to go across the street to the new Fashion Mall and she would meet me in an hour at the fountain. The Fashion Mall seemed soulless now that my mom was out of the picture. The people looked frantic and mean spirited as they ambled around this three tiered mausoleum. I was so anxious over my mom's deterioration I didn't realize there were several fountains and I had forgotten which one she had said. I was suddenly six years old again and lost in a dime store. I reached for my rendition of the worry doll; the CARD. I charged a pair of greatly reduced silver sandals with complicated straps. I never wore them but for that brief time I forgot that my mother was old, really old. Miraculously I found my sister as I was approaching the fountain on the second tier.

Back in Chicago I comforted myself that the nursing home could become a tolerable part of my itinerary if I could get past the smell and stop later at the Fashion Mall. Death never occurred to me because my mother was simply not the dying type. God in all His Mercy knew differently. He knew Marie deserved a heaven and her daughters would survive the trips to malls alone with perhaps a few soft pretzels thrown in for good measure.

Her death was hardly given the pomp it so deserved. Instead it arrived like unassembled furniture mired in agonizing details. There were no Irish bagpipers, no soliloquies from Irish poet laureates or homilies from the Archbishop. But sometimes the bland mundane can be oddly reassuring. The audaciously abrupt plaque on the door of the funeral parlor "Marie O'Malley" was stifling her almost palpable verve. A blotchy faced, slightly inebriated priest officiated at the Memorial. For reasons I can only conjecture my mother was to be cremated without a funeral Mass. My devout mom was poor. I am sure, in all her Irish pragmatism, she would have chosen economy relying on her many hours of Novenas to take care of her eternal reward.

Following the short service there was an awkward interval when everyone felt compelled to mingle. Small talk was taxing. I sidled over to my big brother Jake. While I was talking to him my cousin Celia came up and hugged me and as she rolled her eyes upward assured me mom was watching us from a cloud. I too was looking up to the heavens hallucinating about a comfortable booth and a martini and eventually bolting to the bathroom to regroup. I was having some real apprehension over this memorial. My brother is a good man but in dealing with his chronically poor sisters has had bouts of pecuniary interruptus. I couldn't be sure if he was paying for this or not. Did my brother assume my mother had burial Insurance? And did she? Either way would have been strangely and endearingly characteristic. Did my sister and brother already discuss this? This could feasibly be like something out of a zany comedy with each just assuming the other... Oh God! I stayed in the stall long enough to do some breathing exercises and assure myself that by being a struggling single mother I was immune from this financial fray.

The mourners began to sidle towards the door. Directions were exchanged concerning a restaurant on University Drive. Mr. Wastle the funeral director was clearly agitated. His ruddy neck alternated between ejecting like a jack- in -the- box towards the door and, like Linda Blair in the Exorcist, swirling back around as he kept tabs on the remaining family. I knew there was an issue. His liver spotted hands were trembling as he attempted final consolations. Then suddenly like a scene out of "Cops" the old man was accosting my brother with papers as Jake was getting into his rented car. There was a whispered exchange between Jake and Mary, an obvious huge misunderstanding. They turned around and went back to the "Peaceful Hearts" Chapel behind old Mr. Wastle. I, the nosy little sister tagged along. I watched in utter shock as my sister pulled a familiar piece of plastic from her purse. My God I was witnessing a credit card milestone. My mother charged her own funeral.

Let's just suppose for a minute she really was on that cloud. I think she'd be quite comfortable with the arrangement. She'd probably remind us that life is precious and for everything else there's MasterCard.

CHAPTER 5

Mother

Wednesdays I come directly from the bookstore to my mothers' for weekly dinner. It works well because I go from her usual but somewhat perplexing fare of chicken to a nearby bar for a game of Trivia. But of course like so many traditions the initial reason will long be forgotten and alas, I will be remembered as the single Irish son who worked at a bookstore and visited my mother. Oh God. Anyway it's been a perfect midweek focal point giving mother a project on which she spends an inordinate amount of work and a son a good dinner and enough cocktails for the forbearance to listen to her weekly contretemps. A usual text on Tuesday could be merely "Chicken?" or something like "We haven't had that lemon garlic chicken dish of my mothers in months" or "remember Aunt Dottie's mushroom and honey basted chicken delight?"

Following her martini, which is a genteel euphemism for a heavy handed pouring of vodka along with a few olives, she makes an abrupt and imperious trip to the kitchen. I open the wine as she violently scrapes pans and shakes spoons against bowls. This ritual is followed by plates hurled like discs upon the dining room table; knowing she is on borrowed time. The other night it was barbequed chicken she got from a recipe on some morning talk show. It was dry as hell. She gulped her Pinot Grigio and remarked her usual "What in the hell is wrong with that damn oven. It's from the dark ages" as we are attempting to discreetly masticate the strings.

Understand that I like my mother immensely but her unbridled joy at my presence elicits either sheepishness or downright guilt. Like all mother son relationships I am at once both enmeshed and remote. After a few swallows she might fiddle with an olive and recount some antic back when I was two. She got dewy eyed one evening before an ungodly fare of chicken basted in rhubarb. "Oh Augie, remember Saturday mornings and us in that hide-a- bed watching Popeye and giggling." Oh God! The eyes glisten and the mouth twitches and I look at the time. Equally disconcerting are those moments when she cocks her head and begins by "So what's going on with you" which is turgid with expectations. At thirty five she is becoming convinced that I am slated as the avuncular member of the family, the doting guest in a bow tie and sleeveless sweater vest giving gifts of books on every occasion. I can so clearly hear it: "Be sure and thank your uncle for that lovely book." Oh fucking god! A few Christmases ago she actually gave me a sweater vest and to my dismay SHE was dismayed that I returned it. There are so many bigger perplexities that she doesn't seem to ponder like the fact that I am sleeping on old superman sheets and on my days off I am watching ESPN wrapped in the NFL throw I got for my sixteenth birthday.

After retiring mother adopted a simple lifestyle. She'd like you to think it's very chic and European with a hint of Zen but the fact is she's broke. Another contributing factor to what she refers to as her lackluster routine is that along with her work clothes she discarded most of her co-workers describing them as "Whiney dames who wear too much draped stuff and never giggled." Therefore I have become not only an integral but dire presence in her social cosmos. These thoughts overtake me at the most inopportune moments and I'll find myself wincing on a bus or having a silent conniption fit at three in the morning. When I feel especially guilty for not accompanying her on some damn architectural tour I have to remember that she did the winnowing.

If you met mother you'd see a woman brimming with equanimity but she has her bones to pick. Never a schlepper, she's on the move every day by noon. As she watches fat people board the bus her lips part and she emits a loud reproving sigh. The idea of blaming obesity on anything but eating infuriates her. "Gluttony is one of the seven deadly sins" and her mouth will curl ever so slightly. She also has a lot to say about those who don't speak the 'king's English.' Lately she has a thing about women who anguish over juggling career and motherhood. "Why can't these broads just stay home?" or "Augie! what's wrong with these dames who don't have kids till they're almost fifty, (gross hyperbole)." She yells as we are eating breakfast at the Golden Pancake. This is coming from a woman who loved being home with her children and felt suddenly hoodwinked when her peers were no longer exchanging recipes around a sandbox but instead devising escape plans. She lived in the chimera of a Chicago bungalow with the pungent glow of candles and door wreaths for every occasion. She didn't get the bungalow but now she orders the candles and wreaths from the Home Shopping Show. The vanilla one makes me wretch but I think these cozy remnants of domesticity are her amulets. In the last several years she has also taken great umbrage with technology accusing it of sabotaging her creativity. While she enjoys the computer she cannot decipher between the internet and hard drive and told me she didn't want her writing stored in the sky confusing it with Cloud storage. She briefly tried to find love online which proved disastrous enough for another story.

Last year mother began our evening with another tale involving her financially beleaguered life which never fails to bring on my acid reflux. She had tried unsuccessfully to use her free rider pass. For some reason the machine refused it the first few times and the driver was obnoxious. I was trying to summon the courage to torture some pasty faced endomorphic bus driver when she waved her hand. "No biggie. It finally worked." Following this she "refreshed" her drink which portends either good tidings or an imagined crisis.

"I'm going to be in a documentary."

Years ago mother had known a lady, and I use that verb loosely, who would visit the African import store my mother managed in Evanston;a job not dissimilar from a disjointed succession of quaint overpriced "shoppes" with a double p she managed before she realized the urgency for insurance and 401ks. The woman, Vivian, was loutish and impudent. My mother was helpless, at first reticent to evict someone from a store she didn't own, especially in excitable Evanston, a town that describes itself in its typically abstruse wording as a "a town unmatched for its enthusiastic inclusion" (whatever the hell that means), One morning however, with an overdrawn checking account and a hangover she was besieged by an atavistic territorial violence. As my mother recounted it, one more remark from Vivian finally liberated her of all social compunction. In so many words she told her to buy up or get lost and the lumbering old woman, camera swinging from her neck coat flapping against calves that mother described as bread loaves slammed the door so hard one of the fertility dolls ominously fell from the counter. "Of course at the time that was incidental compared to all the calamities I was facing raising you dear children alone." I suddenly felt bilious and suggested we eat but she continued.

That previous Sunday she had been watching a local news show and she saw a picture of the 'battle ax.' Vivian in all her gruesome glory was now "insinuating herself" into mother's bedroom. But this time she was a star. She thought she was hallucinating when she heard the posthumous praise for what was being described as brilliant photography, The guest, John whom she described as 'looking not a day over twenty' (and this is when I become petulant thinking mother is taking a jab) had won a bid on a storage locker at an auction. From it he had unearthed thousands of negatives. Of course she's thinking I would have destroyed them and she's right. He had diligently developed enough of them to know he had discovered a genius. Yes a genius or as the program's host exclaimed "perhaps the greatest street photographer of the 20th century." So Vivian was becoming famous before my poor mothers eyes. But hark! What was that? John was asking the viewing audience to contact him if they had any knowledge of her because he was going to do a documentary. Mother was visibly and emotionally squirming at this point. She made a third drink and with some oozing from the side of her mouth she recounted her conversation with John who was suddenly her fucking muse. He was coming over in two weeks to film her. I was speechless at my mother's energy; her ability to rise from the smoldering ashes of doldrums. This seemingly mundane conversation with John had transformed her into a whirling dervish. I was sullen as I ate my dinner wondering if this was a reaction to an almost pathological state of boredom. She was engulfed in a sirocco of epiphanies and horizons. I was so transfixed I almost missed my Trivia. The chicken casserole was runny and the cheese topping as stiff as glue which did nothing for my digestive problems.

That next Wednesday was sort of a drag. I guess at heart I'm a selfish bastard but aren't we all? I felt invisible She would gaze at the fireplace ruminating about her possible fame. She floated into the kitchen in a long white gauzy dress leaving a thin causeway of vodka in her wake. There were no napkins on the table. I was taking it personally and barely nodding when she asked about the dinner. How does one respond to leftovers? I left early in the middle of a tirade about her dry skin and receding hairline. What the hell?

That following Wednesday she rudely cancelled, by text no less, saying she was bushed from the filming that day. That Friday however I was more or less summoned to the apartment as if I was having an audience with her. This time I didn't attempt initiating a worthwhile conversation. It was an oratory; a blow by blow synopsis of her interview. She wore the same outfit including the thirty two dollar eye shadow from Nordstrom so I could see it firsthand. I was watching a sort of Show and Tell. She repeated the part of giving them extra batteries for their camera and then wept over her late life self-realization. The chicken was covered with green peppers which are my anathema. I left sullenly.

Mother was clearly under the spell of a new phantasmagoria when she registered for an improv course at Second City. As she put it "I can't return to my parochial life" Caught up in the tide of her new theater life and never one to miss a good soliloquy she used her decrepit cat Missy as an example of her former self.

I attended her first performance and at first I was alarmed. Unlike the rest she was standing on stage stiff legged with hands behind her back like an Army recruit. Among her "classmates" was a hipster who resembled an Iguana with spiked hair, stubby arms and beak face, two girls with hair in dayglo hues and nose piecing, a splay legged chubby guy with a handlebar mustache and two hopping blonds with tattoos. But damn! Mother pulled it off and got the most laughs in a skit as a cat lady. Afterwards I took her to the Old Town Ale house across the street. Even I felt doddering among this young crowd but mother was oblivious as she hugged everyone including the waiter and along with the iguana posed for selfies.

Mother of fucking God. One Tuesday she called to tell me that the damn documentary was picked up by some local theaters, one a mile away. John had actually emailed her regarding the date of the "screening" and reminded her to be there along with family and friends. This was interpreted by mother as a possible cast party or at the very least a panel session immediately following the show, something on the line of Actors Studio. Of course all of this just exacerbated her hysteria. I almost cancelled our dinner that Wednesday after being accosted for nearly an hour at the store by a bumptious mound of jeweled flesh searching for a self-help book with the word 'joyful' in the title. The apartment was imploding with lavender scented candles and mother's agitated breathless rumblings. She knows I hate anything but the breasts but we had chicken wings with some kind of Mexican hot sauce. I was too gaseous for Trivia.

I admit that by the day of the screening I was somewhat caught up in all the hoopla. I was on Clark street a half hour early and went to a bar where I indulged in some Jägermeister induced fantasy about what I would wear to the Oscars and if I had enough credit on my Discover card for two airfares. As I crossed the street from Mulligans I was quickly jolted back into reality by a stricken looking woman teetering in high heels and wrapped in an alarmingly bright geometric print standing in front of the Landmark Cinema. Was she a curiosity?. I won't go that far. After all its Clark street. Her face was an alarming contrast of white and bright pink hue(she told me later it was called raspberry blush by Mac makeup and it "put her back" forty two dollars) and violet eyeshadow. Sunset Blvd came to mind. She was so levitated she tripped as she entered the lobby and loudly ordered two large popcorns to the tune of 15.00. I was afraid for her.The theater was packed. We sat three rows from the front. Mother looked catatonic as the lights dimmed and John appeared on screen. She grabbed my hand when she saw herself say "I never dreamed she was a photographer" and then that was it. Yep. That was it. Oh sure, we sat through another hour and a half but without seeing mother. She has been deleted from the rest of the film. What remained were interviews with Vivians employees and her charges along with some baffled looking distant cousins standing in front of a thatched cottage in a remote part of France.

As the lights returned and the credits rolled my mother sprinted like she did thirty years ago when she imagined someone was teasing me on a playground. We were on the corner of Clark and Diversey once again. She was stoically braving a chilly wind and looking heartbreakingly lovely as we waited for the bus. I put my arm around her waist and hailed a cab. I mean "What the hell, right?" I took her to a Thai restaurant on Broadway and Bryn Mawr.

Life goes on, especially with mother, who always returns to her happy enclave, a dewy eyed revisionist method born of optimistic genes and no doubt nurtured by the 60s with its folk songs and boozy recitations of Kahlil Gibran. She continued cheerfully with our Wednesday dinners and after a few refreshers the tale of Vivian and the documentary became almost unrecognizable with all its high jinx and conviviality. It was therefore typical that mother would end up comforting John when his meteor dimmed several months later due to some legal glitches with Vivian's photography. A few of the baffled cousins had hired a lawyer.

Mother didn't realize that her real gift was not manifested in public but in the Elysium of her still living room where the throw is tossed crookedly over the couch and one plant is always in rigor mortis. It is there when the final shaft of sun still blazes through the white sheers that something majestic happens.

For Christmas that year she requested a cocktail table book on Havana, a place that had intrigued her since she was ten when her parents had taken her there before the revolution. I did one better and got us tickets to Cuba via Cancun, Mexico. I'll pack plenty of my Gelusil. I mean what the hell.

CHAPTER 6

South by Southeast

In May of 2002 I had returned home from Ireland to the apartment in Chicago I shared with my daughter Camille, my son. Augie and my granddaughter, Lily. I was glad to be back but not quite elated. A yearning was not as yet sated. Camille was surveying me in the car on the way from the airport. The last time I experienced this kind of scrutiny was the evening she revealed her pregnancy.

"Would you consider moving to Florida?"

Like I said, the Ireland trip hadn't quite done it for me. The sun was a big factor but the lingering effects of 9/11 played a more significant part in my decision. Proximity to my sister in Ft. Lauderdale suddenly seemed of paramount importance. Two years before I had given up a decent job at a library along with a few IRAs and 401ks to help with Lily. I was poor but not miserably so. The world had evolved mercifully without financial disaster. My resignation hadn't required much deliberation. The drone of complaints and diets had been as noxious as the smells wafting daily out of the microwave in the staff lounge. That last winter while crawling down the Kennedy Expressway I had started experiencing panic attacks.

That evening Camille conveyed the news to our Florida family while I wheezed in bed with a cold. I watched a Discovery Channel show on the Everglades while mentally figuring the expense of moving. Augie decided that it was time to take on the single life without his hovering Irish mother. In addition to my disappointment the pie was now cut in half.

Driving was the first conundrum. Due to some genetic flaw that I rationalize as tradeoff for a creative gene I am one of those faltering menaces that provokes road rage. My dad, a brilliant man, drove like he was driving a pony cart in some Irish folk tale and I am a true urban legend in the graduating class of 1964 when I took our driver's ed teacher for a joyride on the wrong side of a bridge. Thankfully a co-worker of Camille's offered to share the journey for an airline ticket back.

I thought I'd get the most daunting tasks done while I still levitated. Augie and I opened the locker padlock in May. It was a frightening musty testimony to my maudlin affinity for the past. Yellow newspapers were tossed in the garbage without hesitation. But the old toys presented some serious thought. I had to bring black garbage bags upstairs because it was too hot to separate all the stuff in the basement. I would pile a few on our kitchen table and methodically go through each one. I imagined some objects squealing like cheerleaders because they had made the cut and were heading for the Sunshine State. I found the darndest stuff. Why did I have stained Star Wars sheets? Squashed shoes? What the hell?

I won't kid you. My neighborhood had been losing its "culturally diverse charm". Too many pigeons, too much curry emanating from the nearby Indian restaurants, not enough English and its endless winter drabness had taken the bloom off the rose. The lady next door who dries fish on her clothesline is not someone with whom I can exchange pleasantries. West Rogers Park will always be, well, West Rogers Park, home to the huddled masses.

I continued the locker project while intermittently sweating, wheezing and weeping. Putting the Match Box cars in the garage sale pile would be agony. I called my son Brendan, who was married and living in Wisconsin. "I thought you already threw that shit away." was his response. Augie was equally disinterested, texting friends about some concert while I was poking tiny cars in his face. I kept them.

In May we gave notice to our dear but ineffectual landlady, Ellie. We all hugged and cried forgetting the many repairs left undone. Her mantra for 10 years had been "it's hard to find an honest repairman." Ellie decided this would be her juncture as well and put our beloved building on the market. She bought herself a condo a few blocks away with lots of "modern amenities" [dishwasher and central air]. A raspy voiced realtor with puffy lips and officious suit stalked us with prospective buyers. Snotty people were opening doors and making unpleasant remarks about closet space and rotting baseboards. Our haven had become a commodity.

My new credit card (designed with palm trees] had been cut loose like a teenager with a driver's license. Every other day Target bags of glassware, linen and clothing in florescent colors were being giddily dumped on my bed. Camille and I with uncharacteristic and frightening abandon commissioned a mosaic coffee table from a local artesian. Suzy Orman would have swooned.

In May I sold my behemoth antiques to a dealer who was meticulously dressed as some kind of social activist in a flannel shirt, faded jeans, snarled grey beard and wire rimmed glasses. He handed over a measly check along with a wistful long suffering expression as if he was giving humanitarian aid. I felt like I should genuflect at his Doc Martens.

In June I told my ex-husband Patrick and friends that we were moving. No chance now of waffling. We were committed if for no other reason to prove our mettle. In June we had a yard sale. Black bags were hauled to the yard at dawn. People haggled over everything. For some reason, the plastic Xmas holly was a hit with the Muslim women. Strange kids with enormous brown eyes were grabbing Fisher Price toys like Red Cross food. These were the gifts that Patrick and I had wrapped so carefully over the years and slipped under crooked Xmas trees. The old clothes were ignored although I admit there was a vague smell of cat pee wafting around them.

In June Camille got a boot on her car. She never told me the cost of the ticket only that she had to breathe into a paper bag while a city clerk ran for water. In July I bought two airline approved pet carriers for 120.00 and plane tickets for the cats and me. By now nothing shocked me. We just had to go.

In July we attended a 4th of July picnic at Patrick's. The O'Brien family wished us well but I caught a few dubious looks. In July I sold more stuff I swore I'd never sell. I was beginning to have some silent misgivings. It was beastly hot and it occurred to me as I was wrapping my new egret embossed glasses that Florida was always like this.

In July Camille took a long weekend to check out our "Hiatus apt/home" located between Hiatus and Flamingo Blvd. The name itself made me nervous. On the evening of her return she poured me a drink and cautiously warned me of the apartment's square feet. The bedrooms were about half the size of our dining room. She emphasized the walk in closets but I didn't plan on walking around in a closet. I didn't care about the damn island in the kitchen either. I'm not doing a cooking show. What was advertised as a "patio for entertaining" was a slab of cement overlooking highway 84. The lease was signed. We'd sold most of our belongings and our friends now considered us old memories. I tried to keep an eye on the horizon and frantically purchased more tropically themed gadgets for added impetus.

In August a total of eight hundred dollars came due for the table. It had seemed like a pittance when we were in a vortex of zaniness like those dames in old musicals. I was going broke even before leaving the neighborhood. The apartment looked like a meth house. Pieces of furniture were already gone and the bath, toilet and sinks were yellow and gummy. Cigarette ashes were in strange places and tumbleweeds of dust skittered around our once pristine home. I was amazed at how quickly things can go awry. I went to a party at Augie 's new studio apartment in Wicker Park where everyone congregated in the kitchen. The heat and garbage from the back alley and the pending trip made me queasy. This was one of my last nights with him and though it was hot there was that feel of autumn only a Midwesterner would recognize. The voices of children had stilled. There was more shade at four o'clock. The leaves were turning. I would miss autumn in Chicago.

The gritty dirty moving got under way. How could a couch that had been effortlessly delivered not fit through the door again? There was a lot of swearing and gnashing of the teeth. A custom made wardrobe had to be left as well. The top was detachable but on this very hot day it would not budge. A bed corner fell on my daughters toe. She and her friend Ed left at dawn. Camille has an expectant grin as she stood looking alarmingly small next to the truck. I tried to not dwell on those treacherous North Carolina mountains as I look at Ed with his glasses and crooked smile. If they died Lily would barely remember her. All this I am thinking as she clings to her Mom's jeans. I don't want to cry. It will give me a sinus headache for the rest of the day and I have to call Salvation Army and do some serious dusting.

Patrick offered to stay with Lily and me. At first I refused until I took stock of the cavernous rooms. It was not unlike our conjugal beginning. There were ashtrays on some beaten up tables, a TV, two board games and the two of us just hoping for the best. On that last Friday Augie and I took a trip to the Gleasner House Museum, a place I'd been meaning to go for years but never did. We agonizingly attempted small talk. I wanted to be assured he'd be O.K. or maybe I didn't.

Momentous events evoke unexpected thoughts. During the summer some detail or vague smell would hit me like a taser gun. Even the yard sale did not escape circumspection. The saying "Stop to smell the roses" that I'd associated with Hallmark now held a profound meaning and those pesky toys always underfoot had become sacred relics.

We took a taxi to the airport. In spite of the pricey cat carrier pee seeped out onto my lap. Patrick felt compelled to give driving instructions to a very menacing looking driver. At 4:00 pm Lily and I were on Southwest airlines in a capsule with tropical decor that implied promises I prayed to hell it would keep.

That first month I experienced a strange phenomenon. I was lost. My soul was somewhere else, perhaps in the clouds. I had no friends; no niche. I was just another biped walking around in a hot torpor. I started getting what would be described in old novels as the "vapors". My naps were getting increasingly long. One afternoon I awoke sweaty, sad, disoriented. I knew my only salvation was to get vertical. I put on my new pink swimsuit and went to the pool. It had rained. The puddles by the chairs were sizzling and lizards were darting around my feet. It was here that I saw him. Leathery tan and heavily tattooed I recognized him immediately although I'd never seen him before. He is Florida's true State symbol; a hybrid of St Francis and felon. He is a fierce protector of nature and a true iconoclast. He is the hurricane archivist of many identities. His real home is the sand and ocean, the wanton catalyst between the rusty me and the romantic me who loves this hot sneaky place for all the right reasons, my Phoenix rising.

It must be added that the grit, the skyline, the brick three flats beckoned us back. And although we stayed five years we never assimilated. I'm just a feral city girl who thrives on skidding on ice and standing on subways. Florida with its blue sky, warm weather and abundant flora has all the clichés. But life isn't all sunshine and we must preserve our god given fierceness to see us through its tragedies. Chicago is the ultimate allegory. The grey skies and State street panhandlers, the drug addled people in Uptown challenge us, ignite emotions whether kind or malevolent and force us to face our human frailties. The song says the lucky old sun can roll around heaven all day. The rest of us have to work for it and it feels good.

CHAPTER 7

Hummus and Me

My name is Lydia Shaw and I do love hummus. Let me begin by saying that life was exercised with caution when I was a child. Anne, my mother was of no nonsense Nebraska Irish stock. My father, Edmund O'Malley came from a proud lineage of gloomy black Irish who wore their grievances like war medals. Gaiety gave him the heebie jeebies because he saw it as a Protestant imposter. A sliver of levity however visited our household when my big brother John came home on leave from the Marines. For that brief time Dad took his chances with mirth. Mom purchased Coke in the small glass bottles and New Era chips. From the top of the refrigerator the yellow can with its silhouette of a naked woman towered over our oilcloth covered table like a beacon of sunlight.

During my first years of marriage at my zenith of domesticity I was making my own dips including the classic sour cream and onion soup mix which I served in Melmac bowls along with the bon vivant chip of the 60's, Bugles. We would eat them along with our cocktails trying our hand at parent talk while the casserole bubbled in its Corning ware dish.

I'm not sure when hummus came to the supermarket but I would purchase it with the anticipation of a seventh birthday party. And like my seventh birthday when I received cotton panties embroidered with the days of the week instead of the Revlon doll, hummus often came with a downside.

In an attempt to impress my new coworkers at the Northtown library I had invited a few for drinks one Friday night. The idea that I was trying so desperately to ingratiate myself makes me cringe. As a newly divorced insecure parasitic I purchased expensive bottles of white and red wines along with French pastries. I bought tomato and rosemary hummus, Triscuits and a herb grain cracker that promised easy scooping. I had wiped, polished and sanitized. Throughout the apartment were twenty dollar candles purchased during lunch break from a place that spells shop with a double "p". I was sure they would talk about my je-ne-sais-quoi in the staff room on Monday, gushing over my attention to detail right down to the delightful cocktail napkins decorated with martini glasses(at the same 'shoppe' for ten bucks.) But as soon as they had heaved themselves upon my furniture I realized this bunch of duds could not be transplanted. They gathered on my (as yet unpaid for) red microfiber sectional like rescued dogs.I noticed a few craning their necks towards the kitchen. It was clear they were hankering for a real meal. Marge O'Fallon immediately enforced her position as the head of tech services. She heaved one elephantine leg over the other and grabbed the remote. While I was attempting some clever exchange Marge was chewing ice like her cud and staring at the

T.V. Tiny Nancy Smitker from Children's wanted to talk about colonic enemas as I was scooping up some black bean hummus. Rosemary Rigallo from reference was a quiet woman in her forties with an ominous complexion resembling yeast. She wore long dresses that tied in the back like someone who might hand out religious material on State Street. After a few drinks she lit a cigarette. I didn't have the courage to forbid her. Reference is the highest in the in the bibliophile caste system. An hour later she cornered me in the kitchen.

"I have to GET OUT." She looked like someone possessed.

"You can go anytime. I won't be offended."

"I want to get out of my marriage like you did. He's a fucking drunk. I need to stay with you until I get on my feet."

I sobered up immediately. My fright/flight instincts took hold and a shrill unrecognizable voice replied "That would be impossible as my dying mother is coming to live with me."

Someone yelled from the living room that Helen Parger was leaving. I left Rosemary wobbling against the counter like those air dancers in front of car dealerships. I hadn't spoken to little Helen. She was the nicest of the group. She had been a volunteer longer than anyone else had worked there and longer than some had been alive. The director even gave her flowers on her birthday. Helen had halitosis that warranted clinical study. She was brittle thin and her wrinkled little face looked like an apple doll. I was immediately remorseful that I had ignored her in my quest at impressing the rest of these losers. I escorted her downstairs and waited with her until the taxi arrived.Instead of thanking me she said "I have some medical problems. But you'll have them too one day."

Charlotte Switzer from circulation met me on the landing.

"You're going to freak when you see your couch."

On it was a circle of warm urine. I was dizzy. Someone threw a wet cloth on it and soon after everyone left. As I furiously cleaned the couch with every disinfectant under my kitchen sink I was tabulating the obnoxious waste of money on the evening's fete.Helen sent me a thank you note without mention of her incontinence.

Several years later my daughter, Ellen called me to tell me she was coming over from work. I pictured giggles and confidences one can only enjoy with adult daughters. I left the library early pretending I had a doctor's appointment and stopped at my favorite store, Trader Joe's on the way home. I bought a tub of Jalapeno hummus dip, cheese, cashews and Ritz crackers. I had enough vodka for me but purchased her favorite pinot noir. Ellen looked ashen as she threw her coat on the couch.

"Sit down, darling I'll get you some wine. You must have had a hard day."

I swished into the kitchen still dressed up from work pretending I was on a TV daytime soap opera.I heard what sounded like a sob but decided it was my nervous Chihuahua. When I returned Ellen was so lying on the couch.

"I can't have wine now or ever! Ever, ever, ever!"

Edmund's propensity for doom had surged through his loins to me and I was sure it was terminal cancer.

"Jesus! When did you find out?" I was sobbing now.

"When I peed on four fucking sticks."

It took less than a day to go from stunned to Macy's baby department. I ate all the hummus and most of a pizza that night.

Ellen drinks wine again and her gorgeous daughter will be legally allowed to drink it in June.

Hummus isn't always celebratory. When my ex mother- in-law died I invited some of Emmet's siblings over to my apartment after the funeral with the outlandish belief that the families could remain close to one another. As I served the pita bread with dill hummus and a pimento cream cheese spread I was imagining Wayne Dyer lauding my emotional maturity. The two brothers arrived first. Michael gave me a cursory hug.

"Did you see all those people? What an inspiration! Ronny Fastano, the manager of Jewel foods was there. I went to grade school with him.What a fat turd! Gertrude O'Boylefrom mom's Altar Rosary Society sat next to me and had flatulence. Jesus! I thought I was going to puke. Anyone hear what the Cubs did today?"

Johnny and his wife, Sheila barely looked at me. Sheila was shaped like a wedding cake with a small pinched face under a froth of white hair, and hips like the cliffs of Moher. She trotted from the door directly to my food laden credenza. Johnny made himself a drink and sat at the kitchen table crying. I patted his shoulder and he pushed my hand away.

"You don't know what your divorce did to that sainted woman. She couldn't sleep thinking about Emmett. She called me every day crying. Catholics stay together, Margaret. Sheila and I have had our go 'rounds. You think it's easy being married to someone that scrapbooks all day? Jesus! Where's the sex in a fucking glue gun? But we did it. Twenty years next week." He patted his pen protector as if it somehow played a role in their marriage.

Emmett looked ghastly. He stood at the door wild eyed and blotchy faced. He was holding the doorknob, his knees bent as if he was crumbling. He grabbed me and sobbed into my neck. Was this grief or a ploy to reunite? I was uncharacteristically guarded.

"It will be fine. Maybe you could take a class or get back into golf?"

"You don't get it!! She was the only person who loved me for just being me. She didn't care how much money I made or whether I stopped at a bar to unwind once in a while. I don't know how I'm going to cope."

I thought with alarm how a breakdown would affect my child support and how this spread had cost me seventy two bucks.

Their sister, Mary Kate and her husband, Brian arrived with a large cardboard box. I immediately pictured tasty morsels nestled under his arm. Brian with his bald head , round pink face like a newborn, and a tentative tenor voice entered with a stiff legged gait like someone who's just been spanked. Mary Kate reminds me of those wild eyed women in gothic novels who lurk in the castle tower. Brian receives disability for some mysterious ailment and Mary Kate is a receptionist at Our Lady of the Meadow church. Brian put the box on the credenza. Instead of pastry it held hundreds of Mass Cards from the funeral.

"Take as many as you want." Mary Kate announced In a loud melodious timbre as if she was distributing her mother's certificates of deposit.

Fumbling with a pink rosary of Swarovski crystal purchased at Fatima she proclaimed that "Mother has visited me and let her wishes be known. Being her only beloved daughter I am to have the credenza. No need to move the food. Brian and another guy from the church will pick it up tomorrow."

When we were newlyweds Emmett's parents gave us the mahogany credenza and relinquishing it was like relinquishing a pet. It never displayed the intended china. It was a haven for keys ("Did you check the credenza?") school papers, mail and holiday decorations."Not going to happen." A few vodka and tonics gives me bravado "Your brother's children grew up with this piece and I'm keeping it."

Her eyes fluttered and the pupils dilated like someone possessed.

"My brother is an evil entity. He made my sainted mother press his underwear and make oatmeal every fucking morning. She'd be walking up to the Jewel today if it wasn't for him."

Her shrillness and "fuck" out of those quivering lips was unnerving but I didn't relent. With that she grabbed the box of cards and started hitting me on the head. I dodged and the tray of hummus splattered to the floor.

Emmett finally spoke up. "Shut up, you fruitcake! The credenza isn't moving and for everyone's information her little nest egg of twenty thousand dollars is willed to PAWS."

He hugged me and announced I was under a doctor's care and had to rest. Mary Kate, like her dead mother, is enraptured by tragedy and illness. She patted my hand took a mop from my pantry and cleaned up the hummus.

"I'll pray for you" she said tearfully grabbing her purse and some cookies. "C'mon Brian. I have to stop and get milk on the way home."

My family, the O'Malley's were slightly more refined. I knew the ground rules by the time I was seven. Religion, income and politics wasn't discussed. You never asked someone's occupation or displayed family photos and you crossed your legs at the ankles. My mom described the Shaw family as 'rough around the edges.' That was their attraction. I loved the boisterous conversations including the quarrels because I knew they were temporary. My family chooses petulance over yelling. They'd call it decorum. Hurt feelings are nursed in silence for eternity. A rare explanation is both brief and cryptic. They retreat. Phone calls aren't returned. I am relegated to a fragile corner of my psyche to retrace my misstep.

When mom died my sister Molly called me from Florida to relay the news. I didn't cry because it seemed too preposterous that my mother was dead. In spite of being one hundred she just wasn't the dying type. She always went against the grain. She carried herself erect even into old age with a knowing smile that made you think she had the answer to immortality. My parents moved to Florida for my father's health when I was ten but my mother continued to refer to Burdines as Marshal Fields and considered herself a Midwesterner the rest of her life. I am sure they were lonely. They were cordial to their neighbors but in the manner of photojournalists documenting a primitive subculture in the tropics. They had many friends in Chicago but in Hollywood, Florida they were erudite oddballs.

Molly doesn't drive so her friend Joan picked me at the airport. One could mistake Joan for a sanguine soul with her easy phlegmy chortle but she would knock someone out for a flat screen TV on Walmart's Black Friday. Joan is South Florida incarnate. She walks with a swagger and displays a blistering red heart next to Elvis's face on her right shoulder. The memorial service was conducted by a rotund red nosed priest who looked bored and tipsy. As I stood up to leave I could hear a muffled but forceful exchange between Molly, my brother Kevin who was in from New York and the funeral director. Apparently there had been a misunderstanding over the bill. We later converged at a place chosen by Joan and her boyfriend, Joe who manages a Hard Rock Cafe in Hallandale. Vatican's was on Las Olas Blvd near the funeral parlor. A Lazy Susan with the head of a pope sat in the center of each table. My brother a rabid Catholic and a Jesuit groupie looked like he'd been defiled. I wasn't hungry but Molly and I shared a hummus-cheese dip and a veggie tray along with a bottle of Chardonnay. It was shortly after she had switched to vodka that she confessed she'd paid for the memorial with our mothers Discover card.

Thanksgivings like childbirth cloud your memory with nostalgia otherwise you'd never repeat them. They come with a plethora of contretemps from mild, as in who brings the pies, to the tortuous as in who is going to sit at your table and remind you with a sneer that they can't eat dairy and how they've told you that a million times followed by a drunken resurrection of an old wound. But every damn year I roam the aisles of Home Goods Department store dewy eyed as I listen to piped- in Christmas music while looking for Thanksgiving themed dish towels. Last Thanksgiving was a prime example as to whether or not I was a mentally fit individual. In addition to the turkey fare I bought a tray of cheese and fruit and a variety of hummus. I asked no one for a contribution ("just bring yourself, ha ha"). The preparation took a week of baking pies and casseroles. Bewitched by visions of some family (surely not anyone I know) gathered together around a bountiful table saying grace, the men in bow ties, the women with cherubic faces, short pin curled hair and aprons wrapped around their gingham dresses. I invited a distant cousin from Peoria whom I have seen perhaps six times in my life but had recently befriended on Facebook. Dan O'Malley arrived in a reindeer decorated sweater vest and red sport coat which in spite of oven and radiator heat that was enough to incubate a baby chick, he refused to remove.He started on Irish whiskey which never stands alone. It is always accompanied by at least the verbose stage and invariably followed by bellicose and morose. At first his stories were mildly interesting . But alas! They became increasingly more detailed, involving remote relatives punctuated by heavy pauses and repetition as if he were trying to restart an engine. In addition to his increasingly stupefied expression his nose began to run. But he continued to ramble as a string of snot swung like a pendulum from his mustache. In an altered state of felicity brought on by a martini and the Vienna Boys Choir I had invited my widowed neighbor, Marilyn Boyle the previous week. I could tell as soon as she walked into the apartment with a red spandex wrap around dress that she had high expectations. Nothing produces scorn like a disappointed dame. She stood up from the couch weaving slightly from a few glasses of Chardonnay and screamed at Dan, "Does your mother still wipe your damn nose?" With that she went to the bathroom and returned with a box of Kleenex. Part of her dress was tucked in her underpants and Dan started singing "I see London I see France I see Marilyn's underpants!"

Jesus! And we hadn't yet started dinner. By the time we sat at our places (designated by name cards purchased at a Papyrus store for twenty dollars because they had quotes from It's a Wonderful Life embellished in red glitter) my guests were at least somewhat tanked.. My daughter-in-law, Patty, a frenetic wisp of a creature with the temperament of a mother starling was surprisingly calm. I could only surmise she was getting smug satisfaction watching the drama. It wasn't until their daughter, Emily was born that Patty became animated. Her breast milk was an endless topic and she would pull out her breast like a gun from its holster. With a smile like the threaded lips on a rag doll she gleefully helped Dan with his plate and listened to Marilyn talk about the good old days when she went skinny dipping on Easter break in Fort Lauderdale. Immediately following the pie she retrieved Emily from the kiddie table where she sat with her cousins.

"I have to make five dozen oatmeal cookies for Emily's Girl Scout troop so we have to be rushing off."

As I was cleaning up I discovered red wine splattered across the carpet and what looked like yellow baby poop but turned out to be a blob of hummus in the corner of the couch.

Last spring when I was surrounded by sunshine and pollination I agreed to a blind date. I'm in an amateur theater group made up of aged hippies . The women are draped not dressed and wear either too much makeup or none at all. Holly is one of the members. She wears enormous hoop earrings under a pile of gray hair that resembles a confetti gun explosion. Although we had never had an actual conversation she stopped me as I was leaving one afternoon and asked if I'd be interested in meeting a friend of her boyfriend. I'd seen her boyfriend, Butch at one of our performances. He seemed to have hit a snag on the evolutionary scale . But I am always in my own musical. My cerebral cortex must have been napping as I purchased fifty two dollar Channel foundation from a bitch named Miles and a sixty dollar rhinestone bra from Victoria's Secret. The following Friday I treated myself to an Uber for my trip to a dive called Sandy's on Broadway. That should have taken my head out of the May clouds but it didn't. My date heaved himself off the barstool.He wasn't burly. I don't mind a burly man. He had the unbridled fat of a recluse who thinks he has a personal relationship with the characters in a video game. He had hips and splay legs and the chinless flaccid face of that neighbor you tell your kids to avoid. Brad was a security guard at Best Buy but his real calling was extra-terrestrial activity.I chomped on cucumbers and hummus as he related stories of alien abductions. Could it get worse? Yes indeed. While his scholarly side was devoted to the pursuit of aliens, for recreation he was a furry. These are people that dress as animals and attend yearly conventions. My mouth tasted like a furry. Somehow a scab of hummus had found my expensive cheek as I am tearfully remembering that bras are not returnable.

The real story on hummus is the simple one. It is a room full of loved ones. We are all talking over one another. My middle aged children still compete for the floor. The dog is eating crumbs on the rug. I look at their faces and try to imagine life before them, the dog...and hummus. Great stories are veiled in the mundane. It's not vacation pictures but the ones of us on the couch that make the cut. It is those unplanned moments that trigger the trenchant emotion and hummus that keep this world spinning.

CHAPTER 8

ILL Winds Blowing

The two sisters did everything together. Every day it was "I'm going by Adair's" or "I'm going by Ellen's." Everyone saw them as one entity. They called themselves the Bobbsey twins. Since Adair and Ellen were born less than a year apart they fit the definition of "Irish twins." They were from a solid Irish lineage and possessed most of its formidable qualities. They were always slightly on the lam. They were wary of new products and non-Catholics who might "pull a fast one." They resembled characters out of a nursery rhyme with short legs and calves that resembling a milk maid's and large comical faces with dome foreheads that one could cruelly compare to Idaho potatoes Their thin lips were surrounded by random whiskers the texture of a jewelers string but they didn't mind being homely. They honed their peculiarities as a defense against a world they found baffling and menacing. They shared a proclivity for housekeeping. Each had an arsenal of germ killers in their kitchen and would compare brands during their morning coffee. They spent many hours in ferocious attempts at sanitizing their bungalows which were as decrepit as their floral Sears sofas. In addition to cleaning they shared a fixation for soap operas and a love for the bygone days which they carted around like infants at their breast.

They were born and raised on Ashland Avenue on the Northside of Chicago. When their mother Agnes died on the toilet at one hundred and two Ellen and Adair knelt on her front lawn by the shrine of the Virgin and wailed until a neighbor fetched Father Quigley who heaved up the rumpled bodies and escorted them back into the house.

They managed to marry docile men who were willing to keep them together in order to avoid a "tizzy." Emmett and Dan were from the neighborhood and had been altar boys together at St Gertrude's. They had become sufficiently acquiescent after years of a dominating, coddling mother and a sullen father. Emmett was a barber at Sonny's Barber Shop on Clark Street. Dan, Adair's husband had worked for thirty five years at Sully's Butcher Shop on Montrose Ave. The two couples were pedigreed poor. There were no inheritances on the horizon or some germinating 401k's. They lived paycheck to paycheck but took pride in their status as Celtic warriors and blamed everything on the intrusion of "illegals." Being from Rogers Park none of the four had gone beyond Western Avenue as kids except for yearly visits to Marshall Field's or a road trip in the summer and even now they seldom ventured far except for monthly bus trips to Target. Like so many poor chumps they put their trust in the rich Republicans whom they believed spent every waking hour devising a way for the Costello and Connelly family to "get back on track." They considered Ronald Reagan a saint although both couples had a framed picture of John F. Kennedy whom they loved for "his kind Irish face and wonderful family" in their home.

As a part of their deliberate and proud demeanor the sisters adhered to a schedule which was vigorously followed each week. Every Tuesday they would set off with their shopping carts for the three block trip to Jewel Foods loping down the street with their pigeon toed gait ignoring people trying to get around them. After the store they would go to the Golden Grill on the corner where they would remove their scarves, sniff, and cast their eyes about the room in search of any new "elements" in the neighborhood. They indulged themselves with pancakes and their ailments: Ellen with her hip and Adair with her "thingama-jig" which could be a number of things. The sisters thought they were the neighborhood celebrities. They would tease their wait-ress, Gayle about finding her a boyfriend. Gayle dreaded their visits because they were never quite satisfied. "Honey, is this sau-sage fresh?" or "the eggs don't taste quite right" or "more coffee or Sweetie when you have time, a tad more cream." Sometimes as a favor to Gayle, Alex, the manager, would sit with them. The women would giggle and grab his arm while talking excitedly over one another.

One Tuesday the two women were doing their usual visit "by Jewel." They snapped a few beans, squeezed more than a few melons and ate a few Brach candies out of a bin. Adair was first in line. It was their habit to scrutinize the receipts. Regular customers knew better than to get into their line. Today how-ever something else went awry. The bank card was denied. Adair wasn't used to this indignation. She was a veteran at covering her steps. Now she was screaming "What's wrong with you people." Ellen stepped in "Put a lid on it for Chris' sake. I'll pay and we'll figure it out at home."

On the way home Adair's gait was slow and heavy as if she was carrying the cross in a Passion Play. She was blaming technology and the 'illegal alien' who checked her out. Even Ellen was getting sick of her diatribe.

"You couldn't even stop for coffee? What's wrong with you? The world isn't coming to an end so shut up!"

Once back at Adair's, Ellen turned on "her" Price is Right.

"I'm bankrupt and you want to watch people make money. They wouldn't take my debit card and I had to use your credit card for food!" She was crying.

Ellen pulled an extra chair up to the computer and showed her how to get into her account. Adair was as flabbergasted as if her sister had found the cure for cancer. But things went downhill fast. At first the statement was predictable with Jewel, Golden Grill, Dollar store and Target but then came Bubbles and the Hide a Way. Adair did a double take like she was a slapstick routine.

"Go back. What the hell is Bubbles? WHATS BUBBLES?" she was screaming at Ellen.

"I think it's a bar on Broadway and this Hideaway is a motel on Lincoln.

"Holy fucking Mother of god. Where am I??"

"So you never went to Bubbles or the Hide a way???"

All Adair could do was rock back and forth with her head in her hands as if to keep it from exploding.

"Here, breathe into this bag. It will help you. Otherwise you are going to flip out."

Adair lay on her sofa and blew into the bag

"Who else has this account? I'll tell ya who. Danny. And what was he doing at Bubbles or Mother of God, a motel. He never drinks except when he's mowing the lawn."

"Please don't leave me!" cried Adair. "Get me a cold wet washcloth and some of that Jamison's in the pantry that we got last Christmas." The word Christmas made her cry.

"This is not good, Ellen. I wonder who knows. I thought they were looking funny at me on the bus."

"Oh! For Chris' sake. If he's sneaking around it's at night. No one saw him. But I wonder who he was with. I mean he don't do much outside of the neighborhood."

"Should I ask him?"

"What? Are you a fucking Saint? Of course confront him. I wish I could hear the excuses. Like he was entertaining a client. He had to show her his meat. Ha ha."

"Stop it Ellen. I'm dying right here."

"You ain't given' him that satisfaction. He could run off with the whore."

"Listen Kiddo," Ellen put an arm around her sister. "I got some money stashed away. We are going to the loop or better yet maybe Michigan Ave."

"I can't do that. I look terrible and what's the point. A bunch of happy people with money are going to cheer me up?"

"No but I am. We are going to fix your ass so that people think you're a movie star."

The sisters wore what they considered appropriate attire for going downtown. They were swathed in Avon cologne and each had on her best knit pants and polyester floral blouse. They had teased one another's hair into swerving tilted oblivion and covered their whiskers with layers of powder that were crumbling in the heat. For reasons known only to them they topped their cliffs of hair with silk flowers that they had purchased at Family Dollar. They returned the stares with a smile thinking people were bedazzled by their appearance. Every el stop elicited either a memory or an opinion. They raised eyebrows at one another when an African American or Hispanic boarded the bus but they fawned over their babies as proof of their good will towards all.

"Look at all those little braids. That must take a lot of time," said Adair

"Oh! I wish I had a camera. Look at that little lady with all those adorable little munchkins. Why they're as big as she is." Ellen smiled and waved at them.

As soon as they reached Macy's their demeanor changed. They were out of their turf and clearly out of their element. Both started patting their barrettes. Ellen nudged her sister.

"You know we are true individuals. The Irish are gypsies."

Adair took no comfort in this.

"Since when have gypsies been all the rage?"

"Here's what we want." She took Adair's hand and guided her over to a cosmetic counter where a woman with formidable nails and a lab coat as white as her complexion darted over.

"Hi I'm Bonnie. "She ambushed the stunned women. "What can I do you for ladies today?"

Ellen spoke up "My sister needs a lift. You know, maybe some makeup. But she needs a makeover first."

"Oh. Of course. I'd love to introduce you to our latest line of Heaven Sent Pampering cream which you surely will want to take home with you as a part of your fifty dollar required purchase. What kind of skin do you have?" She smiled at Adair; her long arched eyebrows ascending further.

"I don't know. Dry I guess. If your skin flakes is it dry?"

"Oh my! You need help." Her cherry red lips opened and closed like a guppy as she chirped about the importance of skin care.

"First we have to apply this hair removing cream. It's from Spain and you know about those women and their facial hairs. "Ha Ha." The mouth bubbled again. "Now we are going to exfoliate with some seaweed extract that takes all impurities from the skin."

As if Ellen could read her sister's mind she put her hand on Adair's shoulder.

"I told you I'm paying for this. It's my gift to my wonderful sis."

"Oh that's so cute" Bonnie gushed.

Before the make-up, Bonnie applied a coat of whitish stuff that served as the "canvas." She also put on beige "treatment" before applying the eyeshadow. The alabaster face held them in sway like a street entertainer.

"Dan's going to blow a gasket." Ellen looked at Bonnie. "That's her husband you know."

"Well if you're going to make him stand up and holler then you better purchase all this wonderful stuff."

"Like what?" said Ellen. She was getting a little anxious when she tallied up the different products wondering if she hadn't gone a little overboard in her attempt to raise Adair's spirits. "Ok. Here's a list of what I have put on your sister." Ellen felt like she was in consultation with Adair's heart surgeon.

"She has to have the cleanser to remove all that city grime and of course she needs her facial hair depilatory and the Heaven Scent is a must for creamy youthful skin. The foundation is especially geared to her dry skin and the smoky eyeshadow brings out those gorgeous eyes."

"What's the difference between this stuff and Walgreens?" Ellen's harpy side was coming out.

"Well for starters our foundation is made from a secret formula that includes sap from trees in the Amazon jungle. It has many unique and beneficial qualities for difficult skin. Your sister's skin has issues that require special attention. Think of it this way. If your sister had a serious disease you wouldn't buy aspirin right?"

Ellen was abashed. She bit her lip like she did when the nuns yelled at her.

"Yes, that's true."

Adair was starting to feel like a freak the way the two were scrutinizing her with furrowed brows.

"A new face with old hair makes no sense," said Ellen. "I have a lot of credit left on the new Visa they sent me the other day, the one with kittens on it, so hell let's make a day of it."

They were fortunate to replace a recent cancellation at a place on the Gold Coast called Mario's Salon.

"The only difference between a salon and beauty parlor is fifty fucking dollars." said Adair.

"Oh screw it. You have to get with the program. This is why men stray. Their wives get too complacent," said Ellen.

"Well, Emmett behaves himself."

"He's afraid of me and his mother. He knows what'll happen."

At Mario's, Adair was attended to more like an extraterrestrial than a patron. Several men with various neon hair shades picked at her hair like mother apes. Ellen thought she heard giggles from the back room as they discussed Adair's prognosis. A stylist named Trey knelt by her chair and took her hand as if he was pronouncing a death sentence.

"We have a lot of work to do on that little head of yours. Are you willing to be a reckless lady today?"

Ellen emitted a resounding "Hell yes" while Adair sat looking catatonic as she plucked at a phantom whisker.

The ladies returned home by taxi. Adair had a soft bob. Except for the highlights it was reminiscent of her Catholic school days. But now she was wearing an outfit Ellen purchased after two martinis at Miller's Pub; a pair of tight jeans and a cashmere sweater. She did feel sanguine. For once the world seemed less threatening.

"Uh oh. He's home. I'm not coming in but call me later."

"Wait! What should I say? Oh never mind. Screw it. I'll be fine." Adair tried to sound brave but her lips were quivering.

Danny was sitting in the kitchen with his cell phone in one hand and a Schlitz in the other.

Adair stood in the doorway with her hand on her hip. She was trying to put together lines she'd heard on her favorite soap opera.

Danny spoke first. "Did you try to use the bank card today? What a fuckin mess! Someone stole my card and now we have to wait for a new one. Who the hell goes to those Lincoln Avenue flea bags? At least it was caught early enough so we're not responsible for someone else's diddling. "

He stood up and put his hand on Adair's shoulder.

"Holy Moley! You look beautiful."

It was early evening but one last blast of sunlight entered the kitchen window and left a stream of light on her spotless linoleum floor.

CHAPTER 9

Having Their Way
With Flo

Standing in front of Dollar Daily, Flo resembled a crow with her twig legs, sharp nose and a thin black coat covering a body that looked like it would rattle if touched too suddenly. On closer examination one would also see the pinched chalky face, and undulating strands of coarse gray hair that fell just below her ears, an effect produced by pin curls. Lately she had been trying to cut down on her smoking as well as her trips to Stan's Bar on Lunt where her daughter, Erna accused her of being a bar fly. That's why Flo was uncomfortable around women including her own daughter. Women were always advising; scolding and pretending they cared when they just wanted to feel superior. She ruminated over that and Stan's bar as she blew smoke rings up to the grey flat lined Chicago sky.

Flo had been going to Stan's off and on throughout her adult life. But in last five years the patronage had dwindled down to a timorous unsavory group. Toothless Dotty had been "forcibly retired" from a city job and was waiting for some kind of settlement. Tom O'Dea lived with his aged mother who had been aged forever. He claimed she needed him otherwise he would "have had his own pad" years ago. He cut coupons for a hobby and would pass around his rejects ;discounts on wigs, lube jobs and bankruptcy lawyers. There was Bud who had been in construction but hadn't worked in five years with a convoluted explanation about his groin and disability but Flo was usually too soused to follow a story. Cecil Herd came in every day at five. He too had a scantily composed alibi for a life. He dressed in a suit as if he'd stopped in after work but Flo would see him on the Clark street bus at odd hours. Cecil had been in Vietnam and had a fixation for marines and mercenaries. He was always recounting some gory tale from a book or movie. After a few whiskeys he would run his hand through his sparse hair and mutter "son of bitches" to no one in particular. Stan would have to eventually cut him off and escort him to the door. Like Lego figures unless they were safely ensconced within the dank and sour parameters of Stan's they scattered aimlessly and perilously throughout the city's treacherous night landscape.

Flo stamped out her cigarette and went back inside the store when the Pakistani cashier, Rahim knocked on the front window. She wondered how prices were always being questioned when everything was a dollar. But Rahim as well as most of the clientele barely spoke English. Heaven, the other cashier, fielded questions by telling people she was new. Rahim heard her one day and ecstatically reported her to Flo.

Flo and Erna got along miraculously well considering they skirted financial disaster at every turn and spent most of their waking hours silently rebuking one another. Flo felt she could set the world on fire if she hadn't had a child and knew where to light the match. Erna considered herself the head of the household because her job as receptionist for a dental group justified a dress. With her tiny mouth, and pear shaped body Erna resembled a woman in a Reuben painting. But by todays standards she would be considered homely. People never use words like 'homely' anymore and her friends described her as 'striking'. Erna was named after Flo's downstairs neighbor, Ernestine who came to the hospital when she was born and handed Flo a check for one hundred dollars. Although Erna resented the name and criticized Flo's alarming lack of backbone she adored her mother and enjoyed managing her. But in recent years Flo felt there was always something lurking between them as if Erna was trying to convey a secret message which Flo was supposed to decipher. Erna would read self-improvement books and then stare across the living room at Flo who would be watching the Home Shopping Network. At Christmas Flo would find refrigerator magnets with motivational bromides in her stocking. When Flo became manager of Dollar Daily she took Erna to the Red Lobster House and splurged on a bottle of Chianti. But on the third glass Erna told her mother she was limiting herself.

By the time Flo closed the store that evening it was snowing and brutally cold. It was mid-January and the city had become antsy and maybe even a little fearful with daily temperatures in the forties. It was like watching your parents acting silly. Chicagoans want their winter dose of stern weather; the blustery, no nonsense, up by your bootstraps, weather. This is what they expected with their puffy jackets and fur hats, snow blowers and gripes. Flo was feeling energized and needed to "let off some steam." She hadn't been to Stan's in almost a week. Stan was heaving and grunting as he shoveled the snow outside the tavern "Hey Flo you got a new boyfriend?"

"What the hell you talkin' about, Stan?"

"A guy's been in here asking for you."

"Not me!"

"Yes. You. You know an Ed Mc Cauley?"

"It sounds familiar but hell, I'm here a lot and I work down the street. I might have told one of my pitiful old customers about your bar."

"He ain't pitiful and he ain't old by our standards."

"I'm cold and I'm going to have a little whiskey with my beer and think about Ed McCauley. When I'm buzzed things come to me. It's amazing."

She was listening to Bob Overmier's detailed account of his colon problems and the caring staff at Regal Estates nursing home that cared for his dad. He had them canonized by the fourth drink. A subtle decorum suddenly swept the bar. Stan started cleaning the counter and the rest turned to the hockey game.

"Hey Ed! Here's your gal."

She looked into the imposing blue eyes of a reassuring face. Ed was heavy but not ungainly. He smelled of tobacco and cold leather. He took off his gloves and reached out his hand.

"What da ya say, Flo?"

Flo didn't know what to say. She was uncharacteristically uneasy. She pushed her drink back and her bangs forward. Flo had known too many men to distinguish one encounter from the other. They were a putrid, bloated amorphous succession of disheveled half-truths.

"Flo, we met right before I was going out to Los Angeles. We went on a couple of dates. Boy! I was a self-centered pain in the ass. But eventually we all find our way. I made a life; no great California success story but I was happy for a while."

"That was a long time ago but I vaguely remember you."

"Yeh, well, Now I'm here to stay. I just got back a few weeks ago and have an apartment in Lincoln Square."

"Why did you leave California?"

"I got sick of the corporate bullshit and decided to become a teacher. Then my wife left me. One evening I was watching a Black Hawks game and thought 'Shit! What the hell?' It was a scary decision but I needed to be a little scared. It keeps you young."

Flo wanted to keep it going but she remembered one of Erna's many pieces of advice about being mysterious. She had snuck out that evening while Erna was plucking her eyebrows.

"This has been nice but I gotta get going. By the way, what do you do?"

At the present I substitute at St Ida's for peanuts and coach the boys basketball team for free but I have savings. For now I'm doing ok, nothing fancy but that was never my style anyway."

That evening instead of watching Family Feud she sat on her bed filing her nails lost in thoughts of Ed and their future. No one had ever searched for her before and Flo couldn't help that part of herself that saw things as a 50's musical. She blamed it on her Irish roots which in truth had stopped off in Appalachia for a few generations. Flo could never describe herself as lace curtain Irish in the days when such terms were used. They had moved from Kentucky to the north side of Chicago when she was nine. She had attended Saint Gertrude's with the Mary Margaret's and the Kathleen Mary's whose fathers were tavern owners and cops and had the clergy over for Sunday dinners These were the beloved ones with sanctifying grace and plenary indulgences up the ass. How could Flo compete with these kids when she lived in a three flat packed with animal figurines from Woolworths and nothing religious except an dusty palm frond hanging above a mirror in the hallway and a father who told dirty jokes about nuns and said the Vatican was run by highway robbers.

Erna opened the bedroom door. "So did you meet Mr. Wonderful at Stan's?"

"Listen Smarty, you don't think your moms still got it. But how many men are tracking you down?"

She proceeded to talk about Ed McCauley as casually as Flo knew how. "He's nice. But of course, they're all nice at first. Right?"

"Is he going to call you?"

"Of course, you damn fool. He wasn't going to go through all that trouble and then drop me."

"Well watch yourself" and her mouth did its thing again.

"What the hell does that mean?"

"Just don't go getting crazy on me. Start doing some of those breathing exercises I taught you. You know how worked up you can get over guys and it's not healthy."

Flo hated her daughter's attempt at rectitude that was usually at its apex when she was wearing her blue velour tracksuit.

The next day Flo was waiting for Heaven's arrival when a burly, ruddy faced man came up to her and asked where the Kleenex was. It was Ed.

"Hey doll. What about a movie tonight?"

Flo immediately started putting together an outfit and decided she needed to buy one. "Sure but let's make a later movie. I have to do some things after work."

He hugged her in front of her customers. She wanted to dance and sing in the aisles but Heaven walked in scowling and brought Flo's attention back to the store. She almost called Erna to help her shop but decided she'd sooner take a bus than have anyone steal her thunder. Marshalls Department Store was crowded but Flo was determined. She chose a red knit dress. It was casual but sexy and Erna was always telling her to show off her assets. She bought a pair of black tights and black flats with a rhinestones. The line at check-out would have gone faster if someone wasn't trying to take back a worn blouse. The customer turned out to be Heaven. She recognized her screech.

Erna was making meat loaf and acting prissy in her blue velour. "So what's the occasion?"

"Going to the show with Ed."

"Get him to take you somewhere afterwards besides Stan's. And don't let him try any funny business!"

Flo and Ed saw a movie with subtitles at an offbeat theater in Wicker Park. Afterwards they went to a small place referred to as a pub on Halsted Street. Flo told Ed that she had received an associate degree at forty-five from Truman College and realized the world had gotten so far ahead of her she was only offered management trainee positions in retail. She recounted one job at a store in a mall where the salespeople were young enough to be her grandchildren and the music was so loud she was afraid she was going deaf. Ed listened and asked more questions and she didn't feel the need to drink as much. She was imagining Ed helping her put groceries away or picking her up at the airport after one of her trips to see her sister, Millie in Boynton Beach, Florida.

Flo wanted to avoid Erna's questions so she shut her bedroom door and called Millie. She let Millie talk about some annoying woman at the pool and how the Condo association wouldn't let poor Abby Schlinder keep her small dog.

"How could they be so cruel? It's no bigger than a hamster and Abby's been a basket case since Frank passed."

This was so trivial compared to soul mates and true happiness.

"Listen I have some real news. I think this is it!"

"What the hell? You got cancer?"

"I mean I found Mr. Right."

"Well, better late than never. You mean there's still a non ass hole out there?"

"Stan's place was my problem. Erna was right. Who the hell is in a bar but losers?"

"Where did you meet this guy? At Mass?"

"No, Stan's but he's different. He's normal. He does good things like coach basketball and he took me out of the neighborhood and Erna's losing her mind."

"Little Erna always was a Nosey Parker. Remember when I came to visit and she wanted to know why no one in our family had husbands."

"Let's get back to my new boyfriend. I'm going to start a journal, Millie so later on when we do get married we can read it together."

"Shit, Flo. Take a deep breath and get a grip. "

Flo was brooding over Millie's reaction and drinking wine when her phone rang. "Hey Flo, thanks for a great evening. If you aren't busy Friday we could get a pizza and then catch some music at the Green Mill. How's six?"

"I don't leave Dollar Daily till after five thirty and Heaven never balances so it could be later."

"Not a problem. Let's do seven instead."

Flo momentarily lost her bearings and with each gulp she became more immersed in her romantic chimera.

Erna was yelling "Do I smell smoke?"

She didn't answer and locked the door. She had six days to figure an outfit. This required another trip to Marshalls and maybe new eyeliner as well.

She walked out into their small living room at 6:45 the following Friday evening. Erna was shopping for shoes online but Flo knew she was dying to say something.

In the following months Flo and Ed became a couple, a respectable cozy twosome, just corny enough to hold hands as they took their Sunday walks. One Sunday they drove to Long Grove, Ill. Flo was over whelmed by the amount of stuffed bears and potpourri and doors with wreaths and bells that jingled when you opened them. It was called a village and the stores were called Shoppes that sold expensive knit cardigans decorated in kittens and flowers, and other outrageously priced items sold by outrageously chipper women. Afterwards they went back to Stan's for the first time since they had reunited. Stan bought them a drink and the two men talked about hockey. It was so normal it made Flo almost weepy.

They had talked about another longer trip, this time to Michigan. The details hadn't been worked out but Flo got some new tapered jeans and a green turtleneck sweater and some fancy under wear. She thought he would call by the following Tuesday so she would be able to request time off. By Thursday she had not heard from Ed but thought that perhaps their relationship was at a point where he just assumed they would see one another the week end. She worked on Saturday but kept pulling her cell phone out of her pocket. She almost cried when she finally heard her ring tone from The Sound of Music and saw it was just Erna. Earlier she had casually asked her to call because she thought her phone might be broken. She knew Erna was on to her and yet for once she was merciful. That evening the two women went to Target for makeup and later on she said the rosary. By Sunday she was feeling nauseous and afraid a drink would cause a panic attack. She kept reviewing their last conversations and nothing could have been construed as ominous. They had gone to a fund-raiser at St Ida's. She had even had her hair dyed professionally for the event.

She dreaded answering calls from Millie. She didn't want pity and she did not want dissection. She had done that too many times in the past. Erna was being especially nice and that frightened her. That her daughter might consider her mother a tragic figure made it worse. She gave into her old habits and went to Stan's almost every night after work and not only smoked but bummed cigarettes from any miscreant that sat beside her. Stan told her to quit being a "nutsy Fagan." After all hadn't she had practice with this kind of thing? No one in the bar seemed surprised. This was just Flo the chump and her run of the mill losers. Heaven even made a rap song out of it: something about kicken' Ed in his balls. Heaven was now solidly in her corner loving the misery of her company and suddenly they were kindred spirits against their rotten homeboys Ed and Duane.

A talk show host and happiness guru said exercise relieves stress. Flo didn't want to join the Y so she walked everywhere. She purchased a cart and walked to the grocery store, weeping silently down Clark Street. One Sunday morning she was at loose ends. Not having a hangover gave her more hours to fill. She walked five miles to the lake. On the way back she happened to see a lumbering figure in a leather jacket just under the viaduct. She was near sighted but recognized the walk. She turned into the Golden Pancake House and slumped over in the booth like did to as a child when the incense in Mass was overwhelming her. He ambled in causing a small flurry with the Greek manager and hostess who fawned over him.

"Hey don't be greedy." He was laughing as he pushed her over. "A man's gotta put his big derriere somewhere." She was angry at how well he looked and how he had unexpectedly descended upon her. She could barely look up. Her face was parched from a poor diet and tears.

"Hey Kiddo what's up?"

"What the hell does that mean?"

"Well I saw you so out there so I thought I'd follow you in here so we could talk now instead of me waiting any longer and making a production."

"Ed forget it. Don't explain anything. "

"Hear me out for cryin' out loud. You think it's been easy for me? I needed to be alone again for a little while. It's only been a couple of weeks. I don't even know how you really feel about me."

"What's say we go a little further with this thing we got going. You know, like maybe think about marriage or something."

Flo felt queasy. How do you answer someone who has lifted you into a state of divine glory? She cried.

"Flo listen I'm here for you. We'll get a two flat and we'll live happily ever after if I can get you to like hockey."

Flo learned a little about hockey and went to most of the Sox games and pretended she believed they would win a pennant...every year. And Flo got what she always wanted: that exquisite ordinary.

CHAPTER 10

A Southern Breeze

I had just returned from a trip to Ireland. It was raining in Chicago; a continuation of the weather I had been experiencing for ten days. Ireland's grey wet climate is what nurtures its sublimely melancholy writers and the unequivocal charming sangfroid of its people.

But now I was facing my Midwest neighbors and their February vitriol. I had bronchitis and felt decrepit. On the way home from the doctors the following week my daughter Kate gave what sounded more like a PowerPoint presentation than a plan ; a plan she and her Florida cousin, Lizzy had obviously been hatching over the phone for days. She would go to graduate school in Florida and waitress part time and I would help with her daughter. Kate, my granddaughter, Rosie and I were living together in one very large apartment on Chicago's north side, not far from where I was born in Rogers Park. I had left a full time job at a library to help care for Rosie and was presently working as a school librarian where Rosie attended nursery half days.

I have had a long and complicated relationship with South Florida. When I was ten my father had a heart attack which resulted in an early retirement from Sullivan High School and an abrupt move to Hollywood ("By the Sea") Florida. As soon as I graduated from college I returned to Chicago. I was taken by the tropical splendor but only from the sidelines. I'm too pale. I have thin reproving Irish lips made for complaining about the weather and a high furrowed forehead made for winter caps. When we moved to Hollywood in 1955 my dad traded his white Arrow shirts for rayon with palm tree motifs which he left unbuttoned. My mother left her Sears house dresses along with a walnut tea cart to my aunt. I remember the first time I saw her in a halter top. I felt betrayed. They had been such proper people. I couldn't believe they were gradually becoming Floridians. They had taken me from Chicago and Florida had taken them from me. Hollywood at that time was comprised of Italian, New Jersey transplants. Their coarse language was a jolting contrast to my parent's coterie of Chicago friends. My dad's colleagues would come for dinner in bow ties bearing smart opinions and Fannie Mae candy. My sweet mom along with the other wives would remain in the dining room over coffee exchanging recipes and stories about their children. Their gentle voices and the tinkling of their cups were like the sounds of Christmas bells drifting into my bedroom.

Hollywood did not care about books and did not suffer driving fools gladly. They were impatient with my poor parents. It was during a trip to Mass when I learned about "flipping the bird" having mistakenly thought someone was waving to us. Neither of them had driven in Chicago and my dad drove our

1953 Nash like it was a tractor. I was a conflicted passenger; protective and embarrassed at the same time. I dreaded having my mom pick me up from school or the beach. Neither parent understood stick shift and sometimes the car would literally jump up on the curb like it was having a seizure.

The kids at my new Catholic grammar school didn't have to wear uniforms and seemed like waifs with their wrinkled mismatched outfits and reckless pagan names like Gary and Mitzi. I was sad and crabby and developed asthma. At first we lived in a very small duplex. By small I mean the square footage of our living and dining room in Chicago. The neighbors on the other side would come over on Saturday nights to play Canasta. I tried to compare the couples to my favorite TV show, I Love Lucy. But our neighbors were no Ethel and Fred. Penny wore the ruby red lipstick and tight blouses I had seen on covers of True Romance magazine and her husband Bud was a nasally bowlegged cowboy type who wore an ill-fitting royal blue serge suit on Sunday.

My parents purchased their very first house in Florida. It bore no resemblance to our apartment in Chicago with its reassuring sizzle of the radiators, the phone nook and foyer where my mother welcomed guests and hung their coats. The house on McKinley Street was yellow stucco. It had a raised cathedral ceiling on the east side which, like its inhabitants, seemed somewhat out of place and persnickety. Night blooming Jasmine and other exotic growth screened my bedroom window and I had a playmate directly across the street. Sue had dimples and powder white curls and when spoken to offered monosyllabic replies punctuated by giggles. I likened our new friendship to Betsy and Tacy which was one of my favorite books at that time. But Sue's mother wasn't like the storybook moms. Flo didn't talk much. She worked at city hall and returned every evening promptly at five fifteen, her Volkswagen lifting the gravel with fury. The stiletto heels appeared first followed by spindly legs under a dirndl skirt that accentuated her wispy body and, lastly, a maniacal looking permanent wave on top of the ravaged face of an apple doll. She would hop up the steps like a crippled sandpiper. (I was to find out later one leg was shorter). On Saturdays she would drink beer and read Harlequin romances.

South Broward High School was four blistering hot blocks away. I was not allowed a ride by a another student. In my Junior year a grunting sputtering heap of a car driven by Angie Vitalini would pick up Sue. I could hear the music blasting and their laughter as I finished my soft boiled egg served to me in one of the Fiesta Ware egg cups that had made the cut to Florida. I was not allowed to go to the dances in Fort Lauderdale's War Memorial Auditorium where Sue and her friends went on Saturday night. I was not allowed to even attempt to persuade my father who would wince and grab a nitroglycerin pill. Drive-ins were verboten. Occasionally I'd risk his wrath for a ride from school, stopping at Scotts' Hamburger drive-in on the way with Sue and the insatiable high strung Angie who had the looks and brains of a beagle. I'd crawl out of her car at the end of my street and walk the remainder home. I wasn't allowed to attend a party if my dad did not know the family or thought they were "odd balls" which drastically limited my social life but I didn't care. There was a feeling of impending contretemps with these events. I would hear later about boys and beer and cops and girls that 'did it' and just the very thought produced my asthma inhaler. I stayed with my own stricken looking group of misfits who bonded as one does on foreign soil. I was allowed to go to Sue's sleepovers. But everyone laughed too raucously and the mildew in her house made me wheeze. I didn't like Elvis Presley and feigning hysteria was a strain. Flo would intermittently come into Sue's bedroom attempting to be girlish with her Schlitz in one hand and a Kool Menthol in the other, hopping and staggering at the same time. I would yearn for my pink Chenille bedspread; safe and chaste beneath the plastic blue crucifix. Often times I would use the excuse of my allergies and run across the street like an escaped hostage towards the beacon of my sister's profile through our living room jalousies

My dad died when I was sixteen. The leniency I had expected did not follow. The fall after my graduation I was SENT to Sacred Heart Junior College, a women's college in North Carolina. I don't think Catholicism played a big part in my mother's decision. I wasn't a great student in high school and she wanted a place conducive to study. My aunt Loretta, a Mercy nun, facilitated the process. The tepid Holy waters of Sacred Heart were even too prissy for me and it was during the first Easter break that I finally succumbed to the beguine of the palm trees. I did the limbo on Fort Lauderdale beach dressed in a pink bikini while drinking screwdrivers from a Styrofoam cup. In the summer of my Sophomore year I fell under the spell of the night blooming jasmine and a guy from Hollywood who had been a year ahead of me in high school. He played volleyball every Sunday on Johnson street beach with the popular kids and this distinction would sustain his social status as long as he remained in Hollywood. His name was Louie (of course) and he was an imbecile with muscles. We had sex on top of a freezer one night inside his family's Kentucky Fried Chicken in Dania, Florida.

I returned to Chicago the fall after I graduated. I worked in the accounts receivable department at IBM and lived in several apartments on the Near North Side that had retained the accoutrements of their heyday with their crown molding, fireplaces and pantries. One place had a bell situated under the dining room table to summon the help. By the time I was a tenant the bell, along with the rest no longer worked. Toilet handles had to be jiggled and front door keys jimmied. But they held the decrepit glamour of an old silver screen starlet. My roommates and I bided our time drinking boxed wine, reciting Kahlil Gibran on dingy couches with emaciated, tortured looking young men with hair like Jesus until the Friday night in a Division Street bar I found my short haired husband who reminded me of John F. Kennedy.

My sweet mom would pay for my children and me to visit for a few weeks every winter. She would be waiting at the gate (it was allowed in those days) in a pastel pants suit. It was breathtaking to walk out of the airport into the musky muggy air and into the fragrance of my mother's arms. Everyone would be shuffling instead of hustling as they loaded suitcases and folded strollers into cars. The yellow house was my sanctuary. I was still the youngest child when I woke to the soothing voices of my mother and sister. Though I was its fair weather friend Hollywood always had a languid sultry embrace waiting for me. Even Flo would hop across the street the first day of my arrival with a bony hug. Sue and I would have our one evening together; me in prim cotton and a brisk bob and Sue with her Farrah Fawcett hair and sequined boots. On the mornings of my departure I was swathed in tears of unconditional love.

After I divorced I moved back to the womb of my birthplace, Rogers Park. The old neighborhood couldn't shield me from a series of crisis' but at the beginning of the twenty first century I was somewhat solvent and almost alone. I say 'almost' because unless they hate you kids come and go. They gravitate to the nest even if it's a drafty cavern with loose baseboards and an ineffectual landlady. Someone was always half in/half out until my daughter became pregnant and then I had a full time roommate. When Kate posed the idea of going to Florida that winter I saw myself sinewy and tan sitting on a patio burrowed under a entanglement of palm fronds with a few cats and an occasional lizard at my feet regaling a small but formidable colony of South Florida artists. That was the vision that propelled me into relinquishing my Eastlake loveseat, subjecting myself to the torment of a garage sale and the tearful goodbyes to my friends and beloved city.

We found our new home "The Palms" via the internet while still in our Chicago apartment. My niece, Liz had advised us to move into her neighborhood, an area west of Hollywood called Davie because the schools were better. My mom had died two years earlier and my sister, Mary had sold our house in Hollywood and was living in Davie as well. It all seemed to make sense. When one is in the throes of a colossal transition one tends to be somewhat off kilter. Like an oxygen deprived mountain climber I had taken a temporary leave of reason. I could only see those chameleons of my childhood darting across McKinley Street's searing pavement while forgetting how much I hated the searing heat. I didn't really fathom the size of 800 square feet and the patio I had envisioned for my writing life was a slab outside of sliding doors that didn't slide very well. There was a pool and man-made lake where in the throes of my fugue state, I actually pictured myself fishing. It took a while before I realized that without a car you might as well be on an island and, if you included the highways as water, we were. For the first few weeks Kate was driving us to Target and we were spending a lot of time with Mary and Liz so I was blithely unaware of my plight. It wasn't until I walked down a very narrow path alongside highway 84 with an umbrella stroller to pick up Rosie at school that I realized the heat's intensity. It wasn't until I took the shuttle bus from our "gracious gated apartment home" that I realized the limitations of adequate public transportation. Davie's shuttle bus took a long circuitous ride around trailer parks and strip malls ending at a terminal from where one connected to buses going to 'real' places. And those buses were as slow as milk trucks as they meandered five miles and an hour and a half east to the ocean.

I found a job as a substitute teacher so that my hours synchronized with Rosie's. This was following a brief stint in a nearby strip mall on Hiatus Blvd as a tour guide at a children's museum. The place, like its neighbors on either side, Healing Buddha and Cuddly Canines, could more accurately be called a racket. The "mavens of the arts" did not exactly resemble Brooke Astor. They reminded me of the arthritic bow legged sales clerks who followed Sue and me in Hollywood's dime stores. With necks outstretched like they detected a bad smell Gayle and Irene would make frequent rounds of their dusty exhibits to get an idea of the days "take." I met one interesting lady during my stint at the museum. She too was a tour guide and in the mornings we would stand outside and welcome a caravan of yellow Broward County school buses. Gayle and Irene never thought in terms of too many and I often wondered about the fire code. Lynn would always say the same thing in her reedy New jersey squawk. "What the fuck?" as hundreds of children and their flummoxed sweaty teachers filed by us.

Lynn was an excellent water color artist and I was elated to be invited to her home one Saturday evening. I finally caught a glimpse into what I had thought I had wanted. From the outside this was my dream ; a converted three story aqua colored stucco house a few blocks from the ocean. Lynn told me that the other residents were artists as well. Oh my God! I had discovered that elusive colony. But Lynns room had no air conditioning just that charming ceiling fan I had envisioned while I was still in Chicago and damn it was hot. Her one room had a couch which doubled as a bed. I noticed an absence of closets but Lynn pointed to a corner of the room where she stored clothes in plastic boxes. What!? And when she tired of her t- shirts she confided that she would paint them and give them as gifts. What?! The downstairs kitchen facilities were shared with the other tenants. We sat on the roof outside her door which she referred to as her studio. Another pipe dream went awry as I scratched mosquito bites and watched a palmetto bug brazenly squat on my wine glass and cock its head at me. After a few glasses of wine on her "deck/ studio" we drove to the annual Sunset Arts fair on Hollywood Blvd. It didn't take long to see it was fomenting in bad taste. There was a plethora of women in flowing gossamer dresses selling jewelry and florid paintings of palm trees and flamingos.

Oh those flamingos! They were everywhere, drinking martinis to sun-bathing. And the shells. oh my God what they were doing with shells!! Everything from a Mariachi band to smoking cigars and playing poker. Lynn proudly introduced me to Jasmine who had a display of candles resembling genitalia. That along with the heat made me nauseous enough to lie about a sinus headache and make an early exit.

I wrote some short stories from the tiny alcove of our so called "intimate yet elegant "dining area". I loved being with my Florida family and enjoyed being a substitute teacher. But as I sat on the shuttle listening to the mutterings of the passengers and the piped in Christian music (yep) while the driver weighed herself in Publix Grocers I would try to recall what exactly had provoked such a drastic move. It could only be blamed on a horrifying lack of circumspection and that atavistic need to be near one's tribe. Given the day, the weather, solvency and a somewhat viable plan anything is possible. During these moments of reverie I'd also wonder what was more accurate, my self-image of the restless genius, turgid with phrases not read since Tolstoy or just another disenchanted transplant on an aimless bus trip.

I had known before we ever thought of moving that while McKinley street was becoming more than just exotically decadent, the innocuous looking bungalows only a few blocks east of our old house with peeling paint and mold dripping down their exterior were prohibitive. Yep. I knew that. I also knew I didn't like sitting around pools in the afternoon with tattooed nitwits. And very soon after moving I knew damn well that I was never going to be hobnobbing with other writers because I didn't know where to find them and every bus trip called for a complicated itinerary.

That first year in Florida I was involved with job hunting and acclimating myself to my new surroundings. That and lack of funds were the reason for my reticence to return to Chicago. But I was homesick. My best friend Kathleen came for a long weekend. When she left I cried and waited several days before I could bring myself to empty her ashtray. On my first trip back I stayed in Milwaukee with my oldest son Brendan and his family. We drove into Chicago and I saw the new Millennium Park with the giant automated faces gushing water at Crown fountain. It was then I realized the gravity of my mistake like the father who is so consumed by work he misses his child's first steps. It was tortuously sad. How many festivals and book fairs had I missed? During our third year in Florida hurricane Wilma put everything in painful perspective. The die-hard natives look at hurricanes as Mother Nature's majesty and throw a party in her honor. But no one could romanticize its aftermath. The lake where I had pictured casting my rod and cares had become another morning chore. In addition to being without garbage pick-up or electricity we had to contend with our shit, literally. I would take a bucket down to the "dazzling blue lake just steps from your door and perfect for an afternoon of fishing or canoeing" to fetch water for the toilet and hear the melodious refrain of my neighbors "I'll sue those mother fuckin' FEMA people."

The following June, five years after I first beheld the Palms I returned to Chicago. Kate remained for the summer to pack and finish a project at her new job. I took a three month sub-let in Evanston. I had to exert great restraint not to sob as the plane swooped through those last cloud clusters and skimmed the Kennedy expressway. I was home. By this time it was more an escape than a departure. My Florida family receded from my mind. I saw myself back in the reassuring embrace of brick buildings and the recalcitrant jagged streets that lead you on a perplexing and adventurous angle. I was the penitent Dorothy never leaving Kansas again. I was born again and humbly grateful that after a five year absence Chicago still remembered me. I had been friends with Jim, who owned Penn Dutchman Antiques on Western Ave. Across from his store, an old man used to feed the pigeons by the statue of Lincoln. Dozens would sit on his arms and head and poop by his feet. On that first Christmas back I was perusing Jim's store when he yelled across the room "The pigeon man died". Jim felt no further explanation was needed and I was joyful. Of course I knew the pigeon man because I was from the neighborhood and as far as Jim was concerned I had only briefly wandered.

I couldn't love anyone more than my sister but for a long time I was content with phone calls. I was short on cash and she has a tiny place. Even If I could afford a hotel I'd have to taxi back and forth because now I was wise to Davie's public transportation It was like those old movies where the pages of the calendar are turning wildly until the music slows and its six years later. I had to go back. My daughter and I decided on a "road trip". The name connotes a 50's high jinx musical or a documentary where people are cavorting with a farmer or drinking a malt at a diner in Dungsville, Alabama. There were no roadside diners on a highway in 2013 and I couldn't read because it made me dizzy and my allergies were bothering me. By the time we saw "Welcome to the Sunshine State" I was catatonic. I had leg twitches and it was raining like only Florida rains, Armageddon rain where people(not us because we were crazed) were pulling over to wait it out. And then just when my addled brain and stiff ass were shutting down, billboard ads for Wendy's and Motel 6 ceased and we were passing the strip malls in Plantation, Florida.

The next morning Kate and I took a long walk around the Broward Mall because we were staying adjacent to it. Now it no longer represented a stultifying routine but memories of my Florida kin and all the laughter along those corridors. Even the mall's little merry- go -round brought heart tugging memories of Rosie. I took a picture of the Palms and posted it to Facebook with a caption "our old home". One always leaves something of themselves behind and conversely incorporates a significant part of the experience within their soul. Seeing my sister as she walked out her door elicited a torrent of unexpected emotion. The first being regret that I had left her for too long.

We stayed for four days and I cried when we departed. I promised Mary I'd be back in the fall and I will. I'll be back again and again. Damn it, Florida, I couldn't live there but you mean more than just a place to visit. You have Los Olas Blvd. where mom and I shopped for my prom dress. And I can't go down Hollywood Blvd and not see beyond the desperate glitz. The stores have different names but they haven't changed since I was a kid. Sue's grandpa, Sam would take us downtown on Thursday nights when the stores were open till nine. He'd sit on the bench with his New Jersey cronies smoke a cigar and talk about the good old days while Sue and I went to the dime store. She and I were eventually allowed to walk the mile alone to spend our Saturday allowances. We would start our afternoon with a cherry coke and split one order of fries at Ziggy's restaurant. I would put a layaway on some miniature animal figurine in a store that had an 'adults only' section featuring innocuous gadgets like statues with light up breasts or butt shaped ashtrays. It's long since been replaced by a store with preposterous spandex dresses that look like beer cozies interspersed with a smattering of religious statues in iridescent colors. And although Manny's bar has been replaced by a coffee shop that exquisite smarminess still lingers. Irving Berlin is still there with its double knit pants that reach an old man's chin. And Melina's Lingerie where I got my first bra is still in business with nipple tassels and mannequins in a transparent nurse's uniform. Federal Highway may be the scene of drug dealings and prostitutes but damn, once it had me and my dreams walking back and forth to South Broward High School. We visited McKinley street where once I knew every neighbor. Maybe it's survival instinct but kids get the lay of the land more than their parents with their code of bland civilities. We knew that Mrs. Shacky's parrot screamed obscenities if you were anywhere near her yard. And Mrs. Patchulli sat at her window all day while her daughter sat in a wheelchair under a pine tree and laughed with a toothless whinny every time a pine cone fell on her head. We knew that Mrs. Roberts in the pink house with the Blessed Mary statue in front kept her husband's ashes in an urn on the kitchen table and talked about him like he was still alive. We knew that old Mrs. Major drank all day and bribed kids to visit by extending her lead crystal bowl of Brach candy. Old Mr. Gold sometimes pulled weeds with his shorts half zipped and Mrs. Mangus had a black eye every Monday. But all this information was sacrosanct. Either out of some perverse loyalty or fear of restriction we kept our mouths shut. Sue and I walked across that street thousands of times. My little yellow house is now tan but it still holds both the angst and frivolity of my childhood. That northeast bedroom was my fortress and my parents were my palace guards.

Oh! Those days; those days. How can something so common-place become poetry? Almost everyone that dwelled in that tiny enclave including Sue and Flo is gone, except my sister. I love Chicago. It fits my personality. But Mary belongs to Florida and damn I belong to Mary.

Anne is a native of Chicago and mother to four grown children.She recently remarried and resides in Southern Wisconsin with her husband Terry and two cats Trixie and Ace. While she appreciates waking up to the chirping of birds she admits to being an incurable feral city prowler at heart.

www.ingramcontent.com/pod-product-compliance
Lightning Source LLC
Chambersburg PA
CBHW071946190726
48293CB00004B/1375